CLUB MEDS
BY KATHERINE HALL PAGE

SIMON PULSE
New York · London · Toronto · Sydney

SIMON PULSE · An imprint of Simon & Schuster Children's Publishing Division · 1230 Avenue of the Americas, New York, NY 10020 · Copyright © 2006 by Katherine Hall Page · All rights reserved, including the right of reproduction in whole or in part in any form. · SIMON PULSE and colophon are registered trademarks of Simon & Schuster, Inc. · Designed by Jessica Sonkin · The text of this book was set in CharterITC · Manufactured in the United States of America · First Simon Pulse edition July 2006 · Library of Congress Control Number 2005930939 · ISBN-13: 978-1-4169-0903-3 · ISBN-10: 1-4169-0903-6 · 10 9 8 7 6 5 4 3 2 1

For Club Meds members everywhere,
be strong and laugh often

ACKNOWLEDGMENTS

I would like to thank my editor, Ellen Krieger, my agent, Faith Hamlin, and her assistant, Rebecca Friedman, for their support of this book.

Many thanks to Adam Globus-Hoenich for the illustration in Chapter Three.

CLUB MEDS

chapter one

JACK-IN-THE-BOX

I started meds in third grade when Mom came into the classroom to bring me my lunch—which I'd forgotten—saw that good old Miss Delaney had put me in a cardboard box, and freaked.

It wasn't as bad as it sounds. First of all, it was a good-size box. A Maytag washing machine had come in it. I used to be able to recite the serial number and all the specifications, because I spent a lot of time looking at a printed sheet on the inside. Miss Delaney had cut off most of the top so I could see the classroom ceiling, and a hole in the front for me to duck in and out of. She'd made it seem like a special privilege. You may have noticed that teachers do this a lot when they want kids to do things *they* want the kids to do, but the kids themselves know are crap. "It's to help you concentrate. We'll call it your office."

And that's what she did. "Time to go to your office, Jack," she'd say, and give me a math paper or whatever. I didn't mind being in the box. Her classroom was pretty noisy and I wasn't getting much done. I didn't get all that much more done in my office, either, but I could put my head down on my desk and think about playing on the playground with my friend Sam, or draw pictures on another piece of paper until she knocked on the side of the box and told me to come out. It would have been a perfect way to spend the year, except kids started following me around in the halls and at recess, calling me "Jack-in-the-Box" and asking me for burgers and fries. Kids not even in my class, which was pretty upsetting.

I'd learned in kindergarten never to cry in front of other kids no matter what they said to me and not to hit, but when the Jack-in-the-Box thing started, it was hard to stay cool. Sam didn't. One day he got sent to the office for calling Chuck Williams a fuckface and I went with him, because it was my fault too, for being in the box. Our principal, Miss Laughton, didn't seem to get the drift of what was going on and told Sam not to use that word again or she'd call his parents, then she sent us back to our room. Miss Laughton was nice, one of those pillowy old ladies—you know, big and soft looking. She kept a jar of hard candies on her desk and she gave each of us one to save to eat after school.

Then my mother came and saw me in the box. First her face turned wicked white, then red. I'd heard her voice when she came in, telling Miss Delaney about me forgetting my lunch, and looked out of my doorway. Her voice had had a little laugh in it then, but there wasn't any laugh in it later. I'd never heard her use that tone of voice. "Miss Delaney. I want my son out of there immediately and I would like to speak with you in Principal Laughton's office as soon as someone can be found to cover this class."

An aide came to stay with us. Before my mother left the room, she'd told me to get out of the box, pulled my desk and chair from it, and dragged it after her. My mom is a tall lady and plays a lot of tennis. The kids were looking at her like she was either Wonder Woman or Looney Tunes. Then she said everything would be all right, but I hadn't thought anything was wrong.

When Miss Delaney came back, *she* was very red in the face. I went into Mrs. Polk's class for the rest of the year and my parents took me to some kind of doctor and I started the meds. Kids still sometimes ask me for a large order of fries.

. . .

I have ADHD, which stands for Attention-Deficit Hyperactivity Disorder. I prefer to call myself ADD, since I'm not what I'd call hyperactive. I'd like to eliminate the disorder part too, because it sounds like you're mentally ill. My friend Mary, who's also ADHD, says I worry too much about what other people think and she doesn't care what letters they want to call her. She says all the greatest artists, musicians, and writers in history had a screw or more loose. Mary was the best artist in middle school, so maybe there is something to this theory that creativity means being different. She keeps telling me that when we're all adults the popular kids are going to be the losers, selling insurance, in deep-shit credit card debt, with bad marriages and fucked-up kids. We're going to be like Bill Gates or, in her case, selling paintings for millions of dollars.

The problem is that I have trouble thinking about the future. I have trouble thinking about next week, or even tomorrow. When a teacher assigns a paper due in two weeks, I always feel great. It's so far away. Then it's day thirteen and I haven't started it. I hope Mary is right, but it doesn't help with the here and now.

It was Mary who first started calling the nurse's office Club Meds. Her family'd been on a Club Med vacation—you know, where you pay all this money, but once you get there, you pay for everything with beads so you're supposed to feel like it's free.

Then all the kids who went to the nurse for meds got to calling it that and eventually we began to refer to ourselves as charter members and made jokes about where we were going to go for a trip. We've always been careful not to let other kids know about Club Meds, even Mary, who will say whatever comes into her head to anybody, anytime. It's enough to be called hyper, retard, weirdo, speed freak, or sickie.

This year in ninth grade we all have different schedules, but mostly end up at the nurse's office during first lunch. It would be a whole lot easier to take meds myself, but carrying controlled substances around in your pocket is a very big no-no at school. Besides, even with my watch beeping to remind me, I might forget to take them. High school is pretty intense. The halls are even more like zoos than the ones in middle school, and whoever made up my schedule must have been a sadist—or exercise nut. I barely make it on time from one class to the next, sprinting from one end of the building and back again forty-five minutes later. I might hear my watch beep and tell myself I'd take my meds as soon as I got nearer to class, then something would distract me—say, a leaf falling outside the window. It doesn't take much; I can even be distracted by being distracted—and the meds would stay in my pocket. Outside school—at home, a friend's house—I don't have a problem.

It's a funny thing with the meds. A lot of us are taking the same things—Ritalin or Strattera—but we don't act the same, so the pills must affect people differently. We don't talk about it, really—except of course for Mary—but you can still tell. Some kids are very twitchy. I'm a little twitchy myself, like if I'm sitting down I'll kind of bounce my leg. I've noticed a lot of guys do that, though. But the really twitchy kids can't stop tapping their fingers on their desks or picking at some spot on their heads, and their whole bodies seem to vibrate. In elementary and middle school, I'd notice that as it got closer to lunch and time for Club Meds, their rpm increased. In the cafeteria after we'd all been to the nurse, I could pretty much tell when people's meds kicked in. They'd move a little smoother. They'd look happier. They wouldn't be eating much. Ritalin is an appetite suppressant. "Suppressant." When you take medication, your vocabulary increases mightily, and I should do really well on that part of my SATs.

Anyway, you just don't feel hungry. I eat breakfast, drink some milk at lunch and maybe eat part of a sandwich or a slice. Then at dinner I'm starving and it's that way until I fall asleep. Sleep is another thing my meds affect. Ritalin is a stimulant—speed—and can cause insomnia, so I take some other pills to go to sleep. Otherwise I'd be up all night. My mother calls them stoppers and I'm trying to figure out how to tell her I don't need a made-up word anymore, in fact I never did.

My parents, especially Mom, are always asking me how I feel. I guess because I'm growing—but not fast enough; I'm still way too short—and my dosage keeps changing. But it's one of those impossible-to-answer adult questions. I mean, I always feel like me. The meds don't make me feel any particular way. Maybe they did in the beginning, only I can't remember that anymore.

One of the things that really pisses me off about my mom is that everything is the meds to her. If I talk back or get mad at her, right away I see her look at her watch or reach for the pill bottle. She thinks everything is because of the ADHD, and the pills are magic. Teenagers who aren't ADHD don't get this kind of shit. No running for a Tylenol or whatever if the kid slams a door. Don't get me wrong. I'm cool with taking meds. It's just that they're not who I am.

Mary moved into town in sixth grade. Her father got transferred in the middle of the year and she said it really sucked leaving her old school, because at least she knew who all the assholes were there and she'd have to start all over again figuring out who was who. Mary doesn't bounce off the walls—which is what most people think kids like us do—but she says she was a pretty high energy little kid.

As I mentioned, Mary talks a lot, which is good for someone like me who doesn't talk much. At least not unless it's someone I know really well. My parents fall into this category, although it's still hard to talk to them some of the time. Maybe because they always want to talk about things I'm not interested in or plain don't want to discuss. Anyway, Mary says she can tell when her meds are low, when she's getting close to running on empty. She feels kind of restless and if she's in class she really wants to get up and move around. I've had that feeling myself, but Mary actually gets up and *leaves*. I sit and find something to look at to keep me still.

It's not too hard. I have the kind of ADHD where you get super focused. Trouble with transitions. I hear that a lot. Since it's me, I don't notice it, but it can drive the people around me crazy. "Earth to Jack" is what they're going to be putting on my tombstone. If I'm at the computer, I can't stop what I'm doing to do something else I need to do for homework, even if I'm doing something dumb like rearranging my files or fooling around making new icons. I mean to stop, but lose track of how much time has passed. When I'm at school, I feel like I've just gotten the drift of whatever it is we're doing in class, then the bell goes off and it's "And now for something completely different" time. Sam Gold, my best friend, and I love Monty Python. We can recite the entire screenplay of *Holy Grail*. "We are the knights who say ni."

Sam is a member of Club Meds too, but he's on something to keep him from having seizures. He says the pills have no effect on him that he can feel, but he's scared he might forget to take one and have a fit. Everybody would be looking at him foaming at the mouth and rolling around the floor. This hasn't happened since he was a little kid and got diagnosed with epilepsy, but he says there's always the possibility and it would kill his social life forever, not that he has much now, but he's hoping high school will be better than middle school. Way better.

I'm not so sure.

chapter two

THE J-FILES

High school. Specifically Busby Memorial High School. Every normal middle school kid in my town spends eighth grade counting the days until ninth grade begins—high school! Yeah, being a lowly underclassman will suck at first, but you're on your way to the good things in life— getting your braces off, free periods, a driver's license, hopefully sex, or something close to it. Yeah, there's college pressure, but everybody's used to that since it pretty much starts in kindergarten around here. Plus, college is four years away, and meanwhile you're in high school, dude!

But I'm not a normal kid. After middle school graduation—a bogus imitation of the real kind; we had to wear these stupid cardboard caps—I spent most of last summer feeling sick to my stomach. All that stuff about how great high school was going to be was for other people. For me, high school meant Chuck Williams again after a whole year without him. One pain-free year. Physically *and* mentally. My left shoulder, his chosen spot for rabbit punches, had finally stopped aching. I could go into any of the boys' rooms without being afraid he'd corner me and, best of all, I didn't have to hear his lame comments about my appearance—or my being a retard, a freak.

Chuck Williams. I can't remember when he hasn't been in my life, lurking in the shadows to do something, say something. He was even in my preschool. There must have been a year when he was in kindergarten and I was still walking to story time at the library holding on to a long rope with the other little kids, but I don't remember it. Chuck has *always* been around—and always had it in for me. When I told Mary about how Mrs. Williams was super nice to me when we carpooled in elementary school, Mary came up with this whole theory about Chuck being jealous. His mom did used to say stuff like, "Why can't you say 'thank you' the way nice little Jack does?" But this doesn't seem like enough to have set Chuck on his chosen career of making my life a living hell whenever our two paths have crossed.

I do know that he's wrong, though. I'm not a retard.

But sometimes I do feel like a freak. Not like at a carnival, but as in my brain isn't wired the way most people's are. For instance, I'm a pack rat. A teenaged pack rat. Lots of people save things, but I save *everything*. Good stuff and junk. In seventh-grade science we learned about how archaeologists examine middens, the trash heaps of ancient civilizations, for clues to what the people were like. My whole room is one big midden, and I guess you could find plenty of clues about who I am. Me, Jack Sutton.

I have about ten telephones, some working; some not. I pick them up at yard sales; also cameras—the kind you can't get film for anymore. I sort of think the phones and cameras will be valuable someday, but mostly I like having them around and, besides, I wouldn't want to sell them. The dial phones are cool. What else? I went through a Coca-Cola phase and the top shelf of my bookcase has glasses, banks, bottles from other countries, mugs, little trays, and other stuff with the Coke logo on them. Collectibles. I check eBay a lot and some of them are already worth more than I paid.

One of my desk drawers is filled with spare parts, parts that might come in handy someday, even though the remote-control cars or other things they went to have disappeared. I strongly suspect my mom. She claims she never gets rid of anything of mine without my permission, but I doubt this very much. In another drawer I have about a zillion pens and pencils I've picked up in the halls at school. I keep meaning to give them to the library or maybe some other place. People could use them. Next to them, there are a bunch of batteries that may still be good. Underneath are ticket stubs from every movie I've ever been to and used-up Metro Cards from trips to New York or D.C.

Then, in the bottom drawer, I have a lot of rocks. Some are actual mineral specimens and pieces of petrified wood from a trip we made to the Southwest, but most are rocks that I've found on the ground and liked—rocks with lots of mica, or some weird shapes on the surface. One I have has an outline on it that looks exactly like an alien.

The bulk of my room is taken up with computer stuff—yard sales again. Sometimes I get things to work; sometimes not. There's nothing wrong with my iMac, though, and that's where I am right now—in front of it, sitting at the keyboard. Possibly the place I most like to be. By the way, Macs rule! and PCs suck. I love seeing that little smiling icon whenever I turn my computer on.

Mary says I'm too conservative and should embrace all technology—she talks this way sometimes. She also says that I can't throw anything away because I'm ADHD. She started reading about it when she got to middle school to keep up with her parents and find out what she could get away with— "It's not my fault I was born the way I was." I can see her point, but I try not to think about it, and using ADHD for an excuse in my house is pretty complicated, as in my mom would buy it and my dad totally wouldn't. I don't think he even believes it's a real thing. The ADHD, that is. Me screwing up, no problem. That's real to him.

My dad didn't want me to take meds in the beginning and probably still doesn't. After I was diagnosed, I over-heard my parents talking about it. No, wait, make that arguing. This was one of those times I wish I hadn't heard what I did. There are a bunch of these with my parents, but this one was one of the worst. I'm not sure anymore if I really remember it or if I'm just remembering some picture I've put together in my head. Either way, the words that come back are the same.

They were in their bedroom and obviously thought I was asleep, which I was, but their voices woke me up. Mom said that Dad couldn't stand the idea that he had fathered somebody who wasn't perfect like him. Dad said that was bullshit. It was that there was nothing wrong with me. I could pay attention just fine when I wanted to, and the whole ADHD thing was something doctors and drug companies had cooked up to make more money. He didn't want a kid of his to be on pills. Mom began talking about how you couldn't blame someone if he was missing a molecule—I had to look that up the next day—and if I had some other disease like diabetes, Dad would have no problem giving me insulin—these words I knew, because my grandfather has it and everybody was always hiding his doughnuts. They were shouting and Mom yelled that I was going to take the Ritalin whether Dad agreed or not. He slept in the guest room that night and I didn't sleep at all.

But I don't want to think about that now.

Anyway, Mary's a pack rat too, except with her it's clothes and wrapping paper. Whether it's ADHD or not—coins, junk mail, circuit boards, old school papers—it's all my midden and it makes me feel good to wallow in it.

If the house was on fire, what I'd grab would be my computer. It's kind of like a person to me, and a year ago I started the J-Files to write down things I thought were funny or strange, and after a while it got to be like talking to my Mac. I've programmed all these voices and some music, too. While I'm writing, I can listen to tunes or hear Homer Simpson raving. The J-Files are *not* journals. Journals are what teachers are always making you do in school. You have to write what you think of books or just write "your own thoughts." Well, if kids wrote what they were really thinking most of the time, their teachers would shit. I find it very hard to write these school journals, but the J-Files are different, and I write a lot about whether there is such a thing as time travel, like through a worm hole, or sometimes about things that happened to me when I was a little kid. Like flying, which is what I used to spend a lot of my time thinking about before worm holes and computers.

I guess all kids think they can fly at some point when they're growing up. Kids are always jumping out of trees. But I *really* thought I could fly. I must have been about eight. Yeah, eight, because it was third grade and I had good old Miss Delaney for a teacher. Besides having brilliant ideas like putting me in a box, she was a yeller with a wicked temper. She threw a piece of chalk at Dennis Smith one day when he told her she needed a time-out. Usually Dennis could shoot his mouth off and get away with it. Not just because he was big, but he always seemed to know what to do, how to act. Like an adult. He was our class president every year in middle school and is running this year, too. He'll probably keep on being our president until we graduate. Maybe he's in training.

So, I got the idea that if I ran down our hill fast enough I'd get some kind of an updraft that would make me airborne for a few seconds. I used to think about it a lot in class, especially when Miss Delaney was yelling at me or somebody else. I wanted to be able to fly up to the ceiling and out the window. I pictured the look on everybody's face when I flew out of my chair and took off over the trees on the other side of the playground. Everyone's mouth would be hanging open and the entire class would be shouting and pointing up at me.

Each day when I got home, I'd practice my flying. I'd run down the hill, which was a really steep one, then walk back up and do it over and over again until it was time to come in for dinner. I'd do this alone, because there aren't any kids in my neighborhood, only old persons—OPs. They call them that in England, a teacher told us once. I think it sounds better than "senior citizens." Senior citizens—what does that mean exactly? Like you've graduated from being a junior citizen? Old persons, OPs, is what they are.

The OPs around us are nice enough, but pretty busy power-walking, taking courses, and checking their e-mail. I've noticed that OPs are seriously into e-mail. Sometimes I get asked to set it up for one of them. Plus show them how to check out stuff on eBay. They love to do that too, and I'm always happy to help them since I can look at some of the stuff I'm interested in while I'm at it. My time online at home is pretty strictly controlled because my parents think I'm obsessed with the computer. That's also what they said when they finally realized I was running down the hill like a maniac for hours every day.

It was hard to stop. Not hard physically, although it was kind of fun and I was getting fast, but hard to stop believing there was this tiny possibility I could fly. When I'm going to sleep now I can sometimes get the feeling back and imagine I'm floating over the rooftops toward the ocean. And no, I'm not jerking off at the time.

chapter three

TOO MANY TVS

Mary and I were sitting around shooting the breeze one afternoon a few days after school started. As I mentioned, she is a terrific artist. She can draw anything and anyone. In particular, she does great cartoons. I save them, if I can grab them from her before she tears them up. Mary sets very high standards for herself. One of my favorites is of a substitute we had one day. Kids were throwing spitballs and answering to different names, normal kinds of substitute shit, and she called the office. The whole class had to stay after school. Mary drew this during detention and I kept it. I like the way she gave the sub a bat face.

Believe it or not, even though she's so talented, Mary gets lousy grades in art. It's because she doesn't do the assignments—vanishing points and perspective, bowls of fruit. She says she knows how to already and wants to do something more interesting. When she's drawing, it's the only time I see Mary completely still, except her hand is moving of course.

Anyway, we were just talking outside her house, waiting for Sam, and somehow we started talking about ADD. "It's like I'm at Circuit City," Mary said. "You know that whole wall of TVs they have? Every TV is on the same channel. Fifty Pat Sajaks and Vanna Whites, fifty *Wheel of Fortunes* spinning around. I'm standing in front of the wall, but I can't pick a TV to look at. It's not like there are all these shows to choose from—it's the same goddamn show and I still can't watch it because there are too many screens to choose from."

And that pretty much sums it up.

chapter four

BULLIES

I've seen Chuck a bunch of times since school started, but he hasn't seen me. I can't believe how lucky I've been. Neither can Sam. I know he's thinking what I'm thinking: It's only a matter of time before I cross Chuck's radar screen and he realizes the blip is his favorite target.

I watch a lot of those nature shows on public television, and if you learn one thing it's that the universe is made up of predators and prey. School is exactly the same. You have bullies and the kids they pick on. I'd like to think I'm neither, but in life you don't have a choice. The antelopes are always going to have to come down to the watering hole to get something to drink eventually, and the lion is always going to be waiting.

There are categories in all this. At least in my head. There are the bullies themselves, then there are the untouchable popular kids who aren't predators, but sometimes join in with the bullying just for the hell of it. Then there are kids who join in so they won't *be* prey. Mary says this is like people feeding the tiger in the hope that the tiger will eat them last. Then there are kids who honestly don't seem to care. Smart kids. They go their own way and it's like they're just visiting school, passing through before they get a Nobel Prize. Then there's everybody else, especially the Club Meds membership. It's kind of sickening sometimes.

The worst bully in my own personal history has always been Chuck, Chuck the Puck. We call him this (not to his face), because he has been playing ice hockey since he could walk or maybe even before. His dad is a fanatic too, and probably attached skates to the kid's hands and feet when he was crawling. Ice hockey is a big thing in our town. Most sports are.

I am not very athletic. No, make that I am totally uncoordinated. This is a very big disappointment to my father, who was and still is a complete jock. He can't play football anymore, but he runs ten miles a day, and every Saturday he plays basketball with all these old guys his age. He put up a basketball hoop on the garage when I was about five and I still can't get the damn ball in except once in a while by chance. He started me in T-ball, but that didn't work out either. I would really try and we'd practice at home, but I never could hit or catch the ball. I like to ride my bike. I can do that all right, and I'm a decent skier. But team sports are not my thing. ADHD kids can get confused pretty easily, and there's certainly a lot of mass confusion on all the playing fields I've been on. I try not to feel bad, but just once I'd like not to get picked last for a sport. Even Sam, who is a klutz, and our friend Joseph, who's in a wheelchair, get picked before me.

Joseph should actually get picked first, because he's really coordinated and can hit and catch anything. He's really good at basketball, too, but it's the Chucks of the world who are doing the picking and they would never pick a kid in a wheelchair just on general principles. Like they have to remind the kid that's he's different. School is based on this whole idea, no matter how many units we have on how everybody's the same.

Joseph is a great guy and does wheelchair racing on the weekends. He's been paralyzed from the waist down since birth. He has spina bifida. Chuck the Puck and his gross friends used to follow Joseph around on the playground in elementary school and take his spare underwear out of the knapsack that hung on the back of his chair. Chuck would wave it around and put it up real high on the jungle gym. They'd laugh like hell and Joseph would yell at them. Sam or I would get it down, then Chuck would go for us. Dumb fucks. Why couldn't they get it through their heads that Joseph couldn't tell when he had to go to the bathroom because he couldn't feel anything? Or maybe in their own perverted way, they thought this was hysterical.

Joseph had to use a catheter. Eventually he learned to cath himself and stay on a schedule, and Chuck and his buddies found a new way to torment him. Joseph's shirt would sometimes ride up in back and you could see a little below his waist, not his crack, but almost. They'd bring some cool girl like Linda Abernathy up and offer her a peep show. Very nice kids.

My worst year was when Chuck was in my class. Some education person, who obviously had never been around kids much, came up with the brilliant idea of combining grades. I went from kindergarten into a combination first and second grade. Maybe if I take a course in psychology or something in college, the professor will explain the reasoning behind this, but it was pretty much like dumping a whole bunch of Christians—very small Christians—in with those lions. And Chuck was the biggest. Maybe Mary is right and he didn't like his mom comparing him to me, but I think the whole thing started that year when the teacher kept putting him in the first-grade groups. The whole idea of this combined-grades thing is that everybody gets to work at his or her own speed. Sam, who is a genius, was doing all the second-grade stuff pretty soon. Chuck, who is so not, was redoing the year before. And like nobody was supposed to notice. I entirely blame that educator for everything I, and sometimes Sam, have suffered. Chuck didn't like it that Sam was such a know-it-all. But he *really* didn't like having to be with me—not that I was getting the stuff any better than he was. But this is the time when things first started to get intense. He particularly got a kick out of spitting on my desk every day as he walked past. Mrs. Graham thought I had allergies because I was always getting a tissue from the box on her desk, so she gave me one of my own.

I made the mistake of telling my mother about Chuck once—not the spitting thing or anything to do with me; I was young, but not stupid—and got this whole lecture about bullies being the real losers. How they had to pick on others as a way of making themselves feel powerful. It's true that Chuck doesn't get very good grades, never has, but overall I think he feels just fine about the way he is, always has. Plus Mom missed the point. Bullies *are* powerful.

And they never change.

chapter five

VALUES

Sam and I were both pretty excited at the beginning of this year when the gym teachers gave us these sheets to have our parents sign giving permission for us to participate in a Life Skills course. If your parents had to give permission, we figured there was a good chance we'd be learning something new about sex, at least maybe see a decent diagram of the female body. But it turned out to be about "making good choices." I had the class first and when Sam saw my face at Club Meds before lunch, he knew it had been boring. He shook his head. "Values, right? They always start with values."

I shouldn't have written "gym" teachers. We don't have "gym" or even phys ed at Busby High School. We have "Wellness." The point is not to cram some kind of sweaty activity and a shower into one class period, but to "establish lifelong patterns of good diet and exercise."

I think we all know that Twinkies, Doritos, Pop-Tarts, Coke, Twizzlers, and Big Macs are not the six basic food groups. We've been coloring in that pyramid since preschool. And going to the kitchen for any of the above does not equal the recommended amount of daily exercise for any age group. We can all recite this stuff backwards and forwards.

But I'm not complaining. Life Skills is one of the good things about high school. Anything that keeps me out of a locker room with the Chucks of the world is a good thing. And the course this quarter consists of sitting in a classroom plus walking. Yes, walking. We have to keep a log. The other quarters we can choose among the normal gym, oops, Wellness, stuff, plus things like yoga and rock climbing (fake, a climbing wall in the gym, but I'm definitely signing up. Not sure about the yoga. Could be all girls—maybe girls in leotards—and that would be a bad thing because . . . ?).

I've always had trouble finishing things in class and have to bring stuff home to do besides my regular homework. This afternoon I was staring at a Life Skills worksheet. All the time in the world wasn't going to help me. The instructions read: "Make you own Tree of Values. Start with the top limbs and fill in the things that are *most* important in life, then work your way down the trunk. Prioritize and be ready to defend your answers in class."

Life now? Or life later? That was my first thought. I decided to do life now for the reason stated before, that later is virtually impossible for me to contemplate. Most of my friends have their careers all planned out—even Sam wants to go to MIT like his dad and be a physicist. When I was in first grade and we had to draw a picture of what we wanted to be when we grew up, another kid was drawing a picture of a cop and I thought that would be a pretty neat thing to be, so I drew one too. But you can't keep saying you want to be a policeman when you're in ninth grade, unless, of course, you really mean it, and then you'd say something like law enforcement. It's not that I have anything against cops, but I don't think I'd be very good at it, and frankly the idea of shooting a gun scares the shit out of me.

So, life now. What's important? I added some leaves to the tree and asked my mother if I could do the assignment on my computer, knowing she'd say no. She did. The whole obsession thing. This was a short assignment and she knew that I'd do stuff like Google "Tree of Values" and wander in cyberspace for hours. I do most of my homework in the kitchen on a big table under her eagle eye, or as she says, "so you can stay on track."

I drew a little squirrel at the bottom of my tree. Friendships? Was that what the teacher meant? Or things like life, liberty, and the pursuit of happiness? I knew money was out, although not having it makes life impossible. I decided to play it safe and do some of each kind of value I could think of. On the top two branches I wrote "Family" and "Freedom." Family values are very big now, and Mr. Margolis seemed like a family values kind of guy. On the next level I wrote "Helping Others," "Friendship," and "Honesty." The "Helping Others" is not bullshit. It's pretty important to me. You *have* to help others, otherwise there would be a lot of people who would never get through life. A lot of people don't.

On the bottom limbs I wrote "Religion," "Hard Work," and "Health." I have no idea whether health is a value or not, but your life wouldn't be much without it, and a sound body is the first step on the path to a life of wellness, after all—not Mr. Margolis's exact words, but pretty close. He reads from cards. I think this is because all the Wellness teachers are supposed to be telling us the exact same things to start us on the right path. Or maybe Mr. Margolis doesn't like talking in front of a class. I definitely don't.

"Hard Work." I know what that means and try not to think about it. Hard work looms over me for what seems like every day for a million years, no, a trillion. It's shoved in the back of my head with plenty of other stuff for company. Like, will I be able to make it through high school, let alone college? (Not just because of Chuck, but because of things like algebra). Then "Religion." My family is not particularly religious, but I do believe in God. Something had to have started all of this, and definitely something is keeping it going when it seems at times we humans are doing everything we can to screw it all up.

I did not put "A good sex life" on any of the branches, but the whole thing wasn't half bad and was pretty honest. I was putting the sheet in my folder when I realized that my tree didn't have any roots. A good strong wind would blow the whole thing over.

chapter six

MORE VALUES

These Life Skills sheets are driving me crazy. Tonight I'm working on a long list of pairs of words. I have to choose one of the two words and write why I chose it. Examples: I'd rather be a rock or a river, a plus or a minus, a chair or a table, a hammer or a nail. I mean, what the hell?

My mother looked over my shoulder and started laughing, then she came back with one of her and Dad's CDs and put it into the little radio/CD player she has in the kitchen. "Listen," she said, "it's by a group called Simon and Garfunkel." I groaned. My parents don't think any music recorded after 1969 is worth a damn. But I listened.

"I'd rather be a hammer than a nail. Yes I would. If I only could . . ." Mom and I started laughing. We must have played the song ten times. It was really cool. She was dancing around the room and for once I didn't tell her she was grossing me out.

chapter seven

VALUES *AGAIN*

It was a Life Skills quiz. Four questions.

> 1. *Describe yourself ten years from now.*
> 2. *Describe yourself twenty years from now.*
> 3. *Describe yourself thirty years from now.*
> 4. *Describe yourself fifty years from now.*

I stared at the paper for a long time. I asked Mr. Margolis if I could go to the bathroom. He asked me if I was desperate. I had to say no. He told me to sit down and answer the questions. I stared at the paper some more. All around me kids were writing like crazy. What on earth could they be writing about? How could they possibly imagine what they'd be like and where they'd be? The period was almost over. I wrote:

> 1. *I will be twenty-four years old.*

2. I will be thirty-four years old.
3. I will be forty-four years old.
4. I will be sixty-four years old or maybe dead.

I got an "F."

chapter eight
MAYDAY

"I'm sorry! I'm sorry! I'm sorry! I'm really, really sorry!"

You'd think it might feel good to have your best friend apologize, but it didn't. Not in this case. It really, really sucked. And, anyway, Sam had nothing to be sorry for. Well, maybe a little. I mean, what kid brings notices home? He says it was an accident and I believe him. He meant to toss it out, but it was in his jeans pocket and of course his mother found it when she was doing the wash. (A word to the wise, especially younger kids: Never leave anything in your pockets. Your mother will manage to make even an innocent twig that you happened to pick up, because you thought you could use it some time, into some kind of satanic charm or drug paraphernalia.)

Here's the part that is totally not Sam's fault. His mom read the notice and called *my* mom and that's how come Sam and I are going to the "Busby Memorial High School 9th Grade Jamboree. Hosted by the 10th Grade." Sam's dad is driving, so there's no way out. At least he won't have to drop me off afterward, because I'll be in an ambulance. How do I know? Because good old Chuck told me so. Yeah, it rhymes.

I was coming out of Wellness class, racing for English, which is of course at the extreme opposite end of the building, and Chuck was coming out of the locker room. He was smiling. I figured he must have been having a good time snapping wet towels at guys. I ducked my head down and speeded up, but it was too late. I knew it couldn't last and here we were. He'd finally noticed me. He grabbed my backpack and pulled it off. Not only was I now defenseless—the backpack weighs a ton and I could have heaved it at him if things got rough (yeah, right), but my whole life at Busby was now in his hands. All he had to do was unzip the thing and tear up a few papers, like my English homework due in a few minutes, and I'd be screwed. He'd done it before and I could see the memory of those happy times slowly dawn on his face.

"Didn't think you'd make it out of eighth grade, Jackie," he said. "Don't they keep retards back a year? Guess you got lucky."

He knew—and I knew—that luck was the last thing I had. He started to unzip my pack and I was trying to decide whether I should make a run for it or stay and try to salvage some of my belongings once he'd finished making confetti when something lucky *did* happen. A bunch of sophomore girls came out of the girls' locker room and one of them called out to him, "Don't forget the meeting after school about the Jamboree, Chuck." He shoved my backpack at me so hard that I sat down on the floor and everybody laughed when he said, "These ninth graders don't know how to hold their liquor!" Then he went over to the girls, but not before he said, "Don't worry, kid, I'm going to make sure you have an *excellent* time at the Jamboree."

I was late to class and Mr. Rhodes said that as of next week the size of the building and shortness of passing times would no longer be accepted as excuses for tardiness. "When you're in my class, that's my time, so you'll have to give it back to me after school—let's say five minutes for every minute tardy." This is the kind of teacher logic that I can never understand. First of all, it's not his time. Or mine. Or anyone else's. It's just time. You can't own it. Then next, it doesn't do anybody any good to come in after school to "give it back." I doubt he's going to repeat exactly whatever it was he said that someone missed; the first five minutes of class are pretty much bullshit, anyway.

Plus, it's mean. Just long enough so the kid misses his bus, or is late for his ride—very bad if it's his mom (thank goodness I take the bus), and even worse if it's an older kid with a car, because then the kid might not want to drive you anymore, which he doesn't want to do in the first place but his parents are making him because he lives on the same street or whatever and you're coming and going to and from the same place, for goodness' sakes (parent logic, ignoring the fact that neither kid wants anything to do with the plan). I took my seat and thought about starting running again to get my speed up. If I miss my bus, I have to wait for the late one, and that sucks. Plus call home and convince Mom I have to do research in the library. The point is there's no logic to this kind of teacher thinking.

The same thing with the Jamboree. Some principal or maybe a guidance counselor at Busby years ago woke up one morning and said, "Let's have a jamboree ['a large-scale planned celebration with various events and entertainments'; I looked it up] for the ninth graders, put on by the tenth graders so they can all bond and parents will think what a good job we're doing showing the kids how to have good, clean fun instead of getting wasted in somebody's rec room or at the old quarry." They show movies in the auditorium, have a DJ in the cafeteria, and games in the gym. There's food in the lobby. The notices are everywhere. You can't miss them. This year's theme is "Desert Island," like that would be a good place to end up. Especially with Chuck. The whole idea is a *Survivor* nightmare.

Mary says we'll work out a strategy. She's already told me not to drink anything and be sure to pee before I leave home. No going into any of the bathrooms. Mary is very thorough. And we'll stay in a group. Go to the movies, because it would be hard for Chuck to do much there. Definitely no games in the gym or the caf, where the noise would drown out my screams for help. Mary is pretty graphic.

I've thought about pretending to be sick or even out-and-out refusing to go. But I don't like to fight with my parents. It's not worth the aggravation, the hurt looks from my mom for days and my dad walking around as if I'm not there. Faking a stomachache—"You know there's that bug going around"—usually works. My mom is the type who keeps hand cleanser in the glove compartment of her car. But I used this two weeks ago to get out of going to a boring picnic at one of our neighbors' houses where all the kids were much younger and I'd have been expected to keep them entertained. For free. Instead, I spent the afternoon in bed reading *Eragon*, a very cool book by a genius kid only a couple of years older than me.

The Jamboree isn't for another week, so I plan not to think about it until Sam's father honks the horn.

chapter nine
FRIENDS

My mom is always after me to "enlarge my friendship pool." That's what's behind making me go to the Jamboree. Sam's mother is the same way, and I'll bet you anything this phrase got used when they cooked the whole thing up on the phone. The first time Mom said this, I laughed. In my head I saw a giant pool filled with screaming kids, jammed in together, and me on the diving board looking for a spot to jump into. I try to explain to her that I have plenty of friends, all the friends I want, but she wants me to "broaden my scope."

It's true I have all the friends I want. It's also true that even if I wanted to enlarge my pool and broaden my scope, I'd be up shit's creek. The groups at my school have been set since sixth grade or even before, in elementary school. Two middle schools feed into Busby, and it's like the animal kingdom again.

Every species finds its match. At the top of the food chain you have the popular kids. Teachers like them. Parents like them. They look good. They do okay in school, but they're not brains, because that would make them less popular. They're our class officers, on some sports teams, help out in the front office, know what to wear.

The wannabees are next, popular kids in training, and they move in and out of the top group depending on how the popular kids are feeling and how much work needs to be done. The wannabees are necessary for the popular kids' survival. Somebody has to look up to them besides all the adults, and the wannabees are also handy when it's time for car washes and other stuff the class does.

Fund-raising is a major part of school. There's our class's fund-raising—we're saving for a class gift for when we graduate. (Again, not sure about the logic here. Isn't it enough of a gift to Busby that we're leaving and making room for the next class? Instead, we have to buy a tree or a bench or something.) The other fund-raising is selling magazines and wrapping paper for the PTA so they can buy things like computers for the school. I hate to sell stuff, and my mother has enough wrapping paper for the rest of her life at this point. Schools go totally berserk at these times. You're supposed to compete with all the other homerooms and try for these cheesy prizes. My dad says just give them the money, but you can't do that. Last year Mary pissed off her homeroom leader by refusing to sell anything unless she got a cut.

Below the wannabees are the brains, and as I said, they're in their own little world and school is an unavoidable waiting room for the rest of their lives. In a few years, they won't even remember the name of the place. A lot of these kids take their math and science courses at the local community college. One of them did something like split an atom for her science fair project and got to go to the state finals. They also do things like dance with the ballet, solo with the symphony, and exhibit artwork in actual museums.

The bottom-feeders are the druggies, boarders, and kids still seriously into punk. They spend most of their time hanging out at the tennis courts behind the school. A lot of them bring their skateboards to school, and they have a ramp set up down there that they stick in the bushes when school starts. Mary says you can get a contact high just sitting next to one of them, but I think she's imagining things. Every once in a while some of the jocks, a subgroup of the popular kids, will go down there and start calling them names like "faggots" and "burnouts" to start a fight. This is how the jocks deal with boredom. The whole thing doesn't make a lot of sense, of course. It's pretty stupid to call them all faggots, and if someone's gay, whose business is it, anyway?

As for being burnouts, the jocks and all the popular kids are doing just as much drugs and drinking if not more than the tennis court kids. They just do it after school, or on weekends at someone's house whose parents work or aren't home and they're really careful not to get caught. Mary crashed one of their parties once and said they were all puking in the bushes. Hard to think someone's parents wouldn't notice this, especially if the bushes began to die.

Then there's us. Club Meds. I have friends who aren't on meds, but for some reason my closest friends have all been with me lining up year after year in nurses' offices. And if I do make a new friend, chances are there's something different about him. My mom was all excited about this one kid. He wasn't on an IEP, that's a plan that gets drawn up every year about how the school is supposed to help you learn in the best way for your own little peculiarities. She totally embarrassed me by coming out and asking him if he went to "resource"—the name they give the area where kids like me go for extra help. Adults are the only ones who ever use this name. Kids not in it call it "romper room" or other things. Kids who are in it don't call it anything.

Turns out the kid celebrates two birthdays every year, the day he was born and one more year in remission from cancer. He moved away and I still miss him. Mary says we all have special antennae to find each other. Maybe she's right. I can't think what it would be like not to have each other. The druggies may be at the very bottom of the food chain, but most kids view us as another species altogether.

And Mom wants me to dive into the pool?

chapter ten

MY DAD

On TV, especially those old shows on TV Land, when a guy has a problem, he talks to his dad. They'll be in the basement at the dad's tool bench building a birdhouse or in the garage building a go-cart or in the backyard building a tree house. Aside from the fact that we have never done any of these things together and my dad's tool bench is a toolbox, which he almost never uses, I can't imagine telling him about Chuck. Maybe I'm afraid of what Dad would think of me. It is pretty lame to have somebody like Chuck beating up on you all these years, but I honestly don't know what I could have done without making my life even worse. Plus last year without Chuck around made me forget about him, so now it's as if it's all happening for the first time.

This is what taking French was like for me, too, and finally, in eighth grade, I got it waived. "Why make the boy suffer, *n'est pas*?" said Madame O'Reilly, who had probably had enough of me not even remembering the days of the week each fall. (We start a foreign language in third grade in my town, all the better to get into Harvard.) Apparently this is another thing that's hard for ADHD kids—keeping two languages straight— and I'm not arguing. English is tough enough. I do remember *n'est pas*, because Madame O'Reilly ended about every sentence with it, and I also remember *ordinateur*, which is French for "computer."

My dad is a great guy and I love him and I know he loves me back, but we don't have a lot in common. He should have gotten one of those kids who was totally into sports and that kind of father-son stuff. My dad was a Boy Scout until he graduated from high school—an Eagle Scout by that time. We tried Cub Scouts together, but after the second den meeting, he didn't want to do it anymore. I still don't know how I screwed up. I wasn't paying attention and did something weird, I guess. Maybe it was because I kept going to look at the amps and stuff on the stage in the VFW hall where we met instead of learning the pledge and how to tie that handkerchief thing around my neck. We have never discussed it.

We listen to tapes in the car when we go on trips,

and one time we listened to the guy from *A Prairie Home Companion*, Garrison Keillor. He was describing what he thought being born was like—that there was this giant gumball machine in heaven and kids just came down the chute by chance. I ended up with my mom and dad by luck—maybe more for me. My dad should have gotten the next kid in the chute who didn't have ADHD and would have been more like him (and my mom should have gotten that kid who wrote *Eragon*). All in all, I think my dad has done pretty well with his disappointment. We tried going to a couple of Celtics games together last year and at least I knew enough not to ask him any questions. I draw the line at hockey, though. We went to a game here in town once and I saw somebody skate across somebody else's hand.

My dad's job involves a lot of traveling and when he comes home from a trip, he's tired. The way he relaxes is by running. I'm not sure how this works, but he's always much happier when he comes back, totally sweaty. Then he'll watch a game on TV. I'm ashamed to say I don't actually know what it is he does for a living. Something to do with starting new companies from old ones. I think we have plenty of money, because when my mother talks about getting a job, he's pretty definite about our not needing whatever anyone would pay her.

I'm trying to get my dad to go skiing with me. He never learned because he was too busy doing other sports. I'm sure being the natural athlete he is, he'd pick it up right away. He said he'll think about it.

We all know what that means in parent language.

Anyway, there are two basic things about my mom that makes her really different from my dad: She's a worrier—big-time—and Dad and I are the only family she has. Her parents died when she was young. Both of some kind of cancer really close together. So she went to live with her grandmother when she was about twelve. Her grandmother was an only too, and I've never heard Mom mention any aunts, uncles, or anyone except her grandmother, who's dead now. My dad has a huge family, but they all live in New York or California. We've visited them and it's cool to be with all the cousins, but I think they think it's a little odd that my mother doesn't have a soul in the world. At least that's what I heard my aunt Sally say. "You know, Diane doesn't have a soul in the world. No family at all." She made it sound like a social disease, like it was Mom's fault that her parents died and she didn't have a brother or sister. I mention all this because it explains why my mom is so big on our family being together and doing stuff together. I think my dad probably got all the togetherness he wanted when he was a kid, but every year we take a vacation in the summer and again in the winter, the three of us. Mom is also big on all of us eating in the dining room every night and not grabbing something in front of the tube in the kitchen. Even when my dad is away, Mom sets the table and we eat together. This is kind of a pain, but she says I'll appreciate it when I'm an adult. A lot of things fall into this category.

The worrying part must have started the day I was born—or conceived, although that's another thing I don't want to go into. Mary says she always knows when her parents are doing it, because they turn the TV in their bedroom up real loud and the next day her mother always washes the sheets. I have no idea about my parents.

Once Mary asked Sam and me if we thought our parents had happy marriages. Both of us said we had never given it any thought. Sam said he doesn't hear his fight, so they're probably happy. I said I was sure my parents were too. I couldn't honestly say I hadn't heard them fight, though, because my dad does lose his temper—usually at me, but sometimes at Mom. He never hits, but he can say some pretty mean things. It hasn't happened for a while, but I can feel it's there like you're walking on top of a volcano and the ground beneath you feels warm.

When I was younger, I used to ask my mother for a little brother. I guess a sister would have been all right, but I had the idea that a brother would be fun to do things with. What would I have had in common with a girl? Mom always said I was so special, she didn't want any more children, but I'm pretty sure it was Dad, not Mom, who didn't want more kids. I know he thinks having me is enough for my mother to deal with. He pretty much says this when he's mad at me.

It's true Mom spends a lot of time helping me with school stuff. But what are the odds that the next kid down the chute would be ADHD? Then they could have a normal kid for fun and someone Dad could be proud of, maybe a kid who was a basketball star, for instance. The doctor says I haven't hit my growth period yet and that I'll probably be tall like my parents, but even when I do—and it can't be soon enough—I still wouldn't be much good on the court. So I wish they would take a chance and have another kid, although now it's a little late in the game. For me and them. I can't help thinking that if I had a brother or sister, I could stop being mad at my father. Yeah, I *am* mad at him, mixed in with loving him—he's my father—and thinking he's a great guy. But yeah, mad. Mad that he doesn't really know me and doesn't seem to want to try. At least not in any way I've noticed.

Mary has an older brother and younger sister and says I don't know how good I have it. Sam has a sister, much younger, and it's true that she always wants to do what we're doing and she gets into all his stuff. His parents won't let him put a lock on his door—I guess because they're afraid he might have a seizure and they wouldn't be able to get in fast. One time, he rigged up some books to fall on his sister when she opened the door and he got into a lot of trouble, so he has to live with the situation. Maybe I am lucky, but sometimes it's pretty lonely at my house. My dad is allergic, so we can't have any pets. Even fish.

I never heard of anyone else with a fish allergy.

chapter eleven

TEST ON THE HORIZON

I don't know what kinds of courses teachers take to learn how to be teachers, but I think they ought to include one on what kids are like, and more specifically what kids do not think is funny. I have yet to find a teacher with a decent sense of humor, but still they all make what they think are hilariously funny jokes. Like my math teacher, Mr. Schwann. He'll come into the classroom, hold his hand over his eyes like it's wicked bright, scan the room, and say, "People, there's a test on your horizon." Then he chuckles—a really gross sound— and everybody groans or tries to pretend he hasn't done this again for the millionth time. I feel embarrassed for him, and someone should tell the man what a jerk he looks like when he does this kind of thing. Mary isn't in my math class, otherwise the job would already have been accomplished.

The other thing teachers do is call kids "people." Mr. Schwann isn't the only one. Of course we're people, but who talks this way? It's the twenty-first century.

Teachers are very product-oriented. Things like science fairs. For the eighth-grade one, I got a lot of bananas and compared how long it took for them to ripen in a paper bag, in the open, and in the fridge. I took pictures and made a graph—not my idea, but required by our science teacher, Mrs. Moore. It's kind of weird, but the teachers seem to compete with each other. All the time we were getting ready for the fair, Mrs. Moore kept saying things like, "We don't want the other classes to show us up, now, do we?" We'd nod like bobble-heads in the rear windows of cars and all I could think was that this was another example of how out of touch teachers are. I mean, could it possibly matter to us if someone in another class had a more brilliant project? Sam became Mr. Popular for a while because he was going around asking people their favorite color of M&M and passing them out. Red won. Another kid did bananas, but I made all my charts and graphics on the computer. It looked better. He had more information, though. But again, did we care?

The other thing about school is that it never changes.

If you're in seventh grade in this town and it's the first quarter, you have the leaf project, or, as a lot of people call it, the "dreaded" leaf project. It means collecting and pressing a couple of thousand leaves, identifying them, drawing the trees, and putting it all in "an attractive binder with an illustrated cover." Kids have been doing this same project since Noah's time. Seriously. I'll bet the first notebook had an olive leaf. Some kids with older brothers or sisters really have it made, because they can use most of the information over again. Trees don't change. I guess that's cheating, but I have a hard time figuring out whether it's morally justified to cheat when the assignment is totally pointless.

I thought high school would be different. Didn't even hope it would be, just assumed it would be, because it was *high school*. But here we go again. Ninth graders have to make a grammar notebook. Why? We have grammar books for now, had to write our names in the front cover, our real names and not "Dick Hertz," etc., and the real condition, not "worthless." Even in the future if we want to know what a pronoun is, we're going to be able to find a way to look this up without dragging out some loose leaf notebook we made in ninth grade. We don't even really *need* grammar, because we can do a grammar check on the computer just the way we can do a spell check.

Mary is in my English class and raised this point, very politely, but the teacher, Mr. Rhodes, got extremely POed with her and she got sent to the vice principal's office. He was busy with the schedule, which seems to be his main or only job, according to Mary's older brother, who graduated from Busby last year. So she just sat outside his door in the hall. Sitting outside an office door has happened a lot to Mary and she keeps a paperback in her knapsack for these times. She's reading *Lolita* now, just to freak people out. She keeps me informed about what's happening in the book and reads me the good parts. It's pretty funny, but neither of us can figure out what Lolita saw in such an old guy.

I like math, even though it's hard for me. No projects. Just problems to solve and problems you *can* solve, unlike real life. I'd like English, too, if we could read what we want and didn't have to do grammar. When we have labs, science is interesting, but a lot of the time the teacher just talks and it's all in the book, so I don't really listen. Same with history. It's Ancient History and we're doing the Mayans. They seem to crop up a lot. We did them in sixth grade too.

So, school is a bit boring for me, and most of my friends feel the same way. I'm not allowed to use the word "boring" at home. Mom forbids it, because she says saying something is boring doesn't tell her anything. Kids don't have this problem. When we say something is boring, we all know what that means—boring.

chapter twelve

SEX

I'm trying wicked hard not to think about the Jamboree tomorrow night. It doesn't help that Sam, Mary, and a couple of other kids keep giving me these worried looks at school. Plus, I made the mistake of going into the caf for milk and passed Chuck's table. Weirdly enough the reason I didn't notice him was because I was thinking about him. I took off fast, so whatever it was he threw at me missed. Yesterday Mom asked whether the Jamboree was "semiformal" or "casual clothes." This is the kind of question that puts parents in an alternate universe. "Semiformal"? I don't even know what the hell that is. Like part of a tuxedo? The pants, but not the jacket? I told her I'd be wearing something similar to what I had on.

Now it's time to distract myself. Never a problem, and what better thing to write about than sex?

Sometimes I think I'm obsessed with it, because it's everywhere I look. The weather is still warm enough, so at school all these girls are walking around in their little Gap tank tops and you can see their belly buttons and even more, when they raise their hands in class. Most of the female teachers I've had are ancient, but we had a practice teacher in history last year who could have been one of the Bachelorettes. Every time she leaned over to check your work, you could smell her perfume and even sometimes see down her shirt. I couldn't decide if I was glad or sad when she went back to college. It was harder than ever to concentrate when she was around, but by the time she left, I still hadn't seen her whole tit and that had always been my goal. There are some pretty hot teachers at Busby, young ones, but unfortunately I don't have any of them. Maybe next year.

I read this book where the kid watched the teenage girl next door get undressed at night. She conveniently left her shades up and he got off on that, which the author was saying was totally normal. Unfortunately our closest neighbors are the Murrays, and for a start, Mrs. Murray wears these thick stockings Mary says are called support hose—I don't even want to think support for what or, even worse, how Mrs. Murray looks naked.

My dad does not get *Playboy*, which would be a help. Besides *Time*, he gets *Sports Illustrated*, but somehow the swimsuit issue never ends up on the coffee table or anywhere else in the house that I've been able to discover. My mom gets *House Beautiful* and *The New Yorker*, not much help there, either, although sometimes *The New Yorker* has pretty sexy Calvin Klein ads. We do get an amazing number of catalogs, but none for Victoria's Secret. My mother gets one from some Swedish clothing company, and this was promising, but the underwear is all 100 percent natural fibers and looks like something nuns might wear, so even though the models are babes, it's a turnoff.

Mary is much more plugged into who's doing it at school and who isn't—the majority—and I'm a little doubtful that some of the people she says are doing it really are. But Dennis Smith is all over Linda Abernathy at her locker with his tongue down her throat and his hands up her shirt, so it's pretty safe to say they're doing it. Plus Dennis is always smiling a lot. They're careful not to get caught making out at school, though. Kids aren't even allowed to walk down the hall with their hands in each other's back pockets. I don't know what the point of this kind of rule is. Do they think kids without boyfriends or girlfriends feel bad when they see the popular kids all over each other? Or more likely, is it because they think feeling someone's buns in the hall is inappropriate?

This is the kind of question Mary talks about all the time, and she'd ask our principal, Ms. McConnelly, if the woman ever came out of her office. I've been in this school weeks now and have only seen her at the one assembly we've had—the dumb "Welcome to Busby" one. Kids call her "the Phantom" and Mary swears her brother *never* saw her until graduation. And, of course, Mr. Dolan, the vice principal, is busy with his scheduling, which is obviously a major job. At the start of the year, I had three periods of Wellness a day. And this was a minor screw-up compared to some. So he's spending all that time on the schedule doing what, exactly?

Sam and I rented that Woody Allen movie, *Everything You Always Wanted to Know About Sex*, one night when our parents went out together, and it was really funny but not too instructional, although we hadn't known that people were attracted to sheep, and don't much understand it except in the crudest form.

Mary says if we haven't had sex with anyone else by the time we're out of high school, we should have sex with each other. She doesn't want to graduate a virgin, for some reason. I have not given her a final answer, but she told me I have to decide soon, because if I don't want to, she'll ask someone else. I've been thinking of saying yes just to keep her from asking another boy. I don't know why, but the idea gets me upset.

My mother keeps saying that Mary is going to be really beautiful, and when I told Mary that, she burst into tears. She's pretty emotional. Right now she still has to wear a retainer, and her chest is as flat as a board. But she's got nice skin, and her hair is long and shiny. She washes it before school every day. It's brown—"mousy brown," Mary calls it—and she wants to streak it with blond highlights, but her mother would kill her. Her mother wouldn't let her get her ears pierced, either, so Mary did it herself with a darning needle and they got all infected. Her mother said it was body mutilation, but she gave in and, after they healed, let Mary get it done properly. Mary says her mother's always checking her for tattoos and other body piercing. "A strip search in my own home!" she says. I think what someone wants to do with her body is her own business, but some kids do go a little far. Mary once told me that you never see a pretty girl with orange or purple hair and seventeen rings in her lips and tongue. After she said this, I began to notice that she was right. The pretty girls all have maybe two, three holes in their ears and that's it. And they don't dye their hair weird colors.

In seventh grade Mary thought we ought to see what each other looked like naked, but I didn't feel like it at the time and still don't. Mary has no problem leafing through the magazines at the big newsstand in the middle of Harvard Square, and I know that there's no way I come close to those guys except that we all have the same XY chromosome. I've started getting pubic hair, but at the moment the only way anyone could tell would be to feel those wisps, and I'm not about to let Mary do that, although she'd probably be all for it. Dennis Smith always took a shower after gym class and walked around buck naked. Even in eighth grade he had so much hair on his chest, you could practically braid it.

Sometimes Sam and I come close to talking about sex, but it feels weird and we go back to talking about computers or Monty Python or school. Sam jerks off a lot too, he did tell me once, so at least I know that I'm not alone in that. I wouldn't think so anyway, not listening to the way guys tease each other in the locker room. I'm talking about the jocks. Duh.

chapter thirteen

IN THE DARK

I'm home. In one piece. For now, anyway.

The night started out okay. Sam's dad dropped us off and there were a ton of kids outside waiting to show their school IDs, get their hands stamped, and get in, but no sign of Chuck or any of his buddies.

We stood around all jammed together for the Jamboree, which may be where they got the name, but somehow I don't think so. This was fine with me, since a key to survival in school is not standing out. The way you dress, for instance. I stick to jeans and T-shirts that are gray, white, or black without anything on front like a picture of some animal or a place my family has visited. This year, my mother got me a new shirt for the first day of school with a quote from some guy named Henry David Thoreau: "Beware of all enterprises that require new clothes."

I got the message and it's pretty cool, but a shirt with a message is like carrying a loaded gun. Even an okay message like that one. The teachers wouldn't really notice, but kids would and I'd hear about it for the rest of my school career—"Got any new clothes, Jack? Beware what you wear!" Or worse.

The other kinds of T-shirts with messages—"Life Sucks," "Shit Happens," that kind of thing—are banned, and if you wear one, you get suspended. Teachers *do* notice those. It's like they have X-ray vision; they can even spot them under another shirt. The druggies all wear black Kurt Cobain or Metallica concert shirts. There was talk of banning those, too, but nothing has come of it so far.

Tonight I wore a gray T-shirt with a tiny Champion logo (the new shirt is on my closet shelf along with the flannel pajamas I get every year from "Santa"—my grandparents). Mary won't wear any clothes with logos. She says she doesn't see why she should be a walking advertisement for Abercrombie & Fitch or Tommy Hilfiger. They're not paying her; she's shelling out. Most kids do not have this attitude. Anyway, I blended in, and with Sam on one side and Mary on the other as we went through the door, I felt like one of those cowboys in old movies who hold on to the stirrups and hide between two galloping horses.

Once inside, we went straight to the auditorium and pissed a lot of people off by taking three seats in the middle of a crowded row. The movie had already started. *Halloween* some number. I would have preferred a comedy. One of the Pythons. But apparently the tenth grade thought they could bond best with us by scaring the shit out of us. At least it wasn't one of the *Chucky* movies. I don't think I could have handled that. I settled back and let my mind go blank.

After it ended, the lights went on and I hunched way over in my seat. Mary thought I should get down on the floor, but kids were looking at me strangely enough. Sam went to the caf and smuggled in some chocolate chip cookies—no food allowed in the auditorium; the lights went out and it was time for movie number two. I was beginning to feel better. The Jamboree went until midnight, so that meant just one more movie and I'd be home free. A part of me, a big part, wanted to be home *now*, but once you were in the building, you couldn't leave unless a parent came to get you. This was to keep kids from getting tanked at somebody's house nearby and coming back in. Sam said there wasn't any punch in the caf, only cans of soda. So even if you did manage to get a few nips in up your jacket sleeves, you couldn't spike much. Schools spend a lot of time trying to outwit kids, but it's pretty hopeless. Mary told me that she'd heard a lot of kids had stashed stuff in their lockers during the week. We weren't supposed to go to them, but the teacher chaperones couldn't be everywhere.

The next movie was *The Shining*. This was one of those times when I knew who my friends are, because Sam does not like this movie at all. I told him to go back to the caf, that it was okay. I mean, what could Chuck do to me in the dark with all these kids around? Plenty, but at least I'd be hard to find away from the aisles. Sam refused to leave. What a friend.

Crazed Jack Nicholson was filling the screen. He had a hatchet in his hand. "All work and no play makes Jack a dull boy!" I heard Sam gasp and was just about to tell him he really should go when an arm came from behind and wrapped itself around my windpipe.

"You can run, but you can't hide," Chuck whispered in my ear. He'd obviously been one of the kids with a stash somewhere, because his breath smelled like booze.

Mary was pounding on his arm and telling him to leave me alone, but he just shoved her away with his free hand and kids were saying, "Shut the fuck up" because it was such a good part. I wasn't saying anything. Just gurgling and if the auditorium hadn't been black to start with, it would have been going black now. I was kind of aware that Sam was trying to get Chuck to stop and then miraculously his grip loosened. But it wasn't because of Sam. One of the teachers—who were all sitting together in the back like that was going to be a good way to keep an eye on things—finally realized all the action wasn't on the screen and stood up. "People (there it was again), if you're not going to watch the film (teachers always say "film," not "movie"), you *must* leave the auditorium."

"Meet me in the equipment room Monday after school, douchebag. Know where that is?" My ear was feeling hot from his breath.

I nodded. The equipment room was where kids got beat up pretty regularly. There was no way I could make my bus if I met him. There was no way I'd ever be taking a bus again if I didn't.

And that was my Jamboree.

chapter fourteen

A BIG PROBLEM

The weekend passed by way too fast and when I wasn't sleeping, which I tried to do a lot, so I wouldn't have to think, I was IMing with Sam and Mary. This is way better than the phone, since my parents *always* answer on the first ring and if it's for me *always* want to know what the person wanted. I don't ask them that when their friends call, not that I'd be interested. But it's a privacy issue, a one-way street at my house.

I was at my locker before school on Monday morning. There was no point in staying home, or cutting. Chuck was right. I could run, but I couldn't hide. He'd catch up to me even if it wasn't until we were both old guys. I was thinking about this when Chuck suddenly jumped in front of me like some sort of commando and pushed me against the lockers. There wasn't a single teacher or administrator around. They must grab their free time whenever they can, I always figured, because before school, at every lunch period, and after school, there's nobody but kids. Except at lunch if you count the cafeteria workers, who we all know hate kids and with good reason, since they see us at our very worst—food fights, a 150-decibel noise level, and general rowdiness.

"I've been waiting for you, shithead."

Chuck put his hand up next to my face and leaned in toward the wall. His whole body was a few inches from mine. I could smell Right Guard. He could smell fear.

"Hey, weirdo! I'm talking to you!"

I hadn't realized I was supposed to respond. I nodded quickly. He smiled. He has perfect teeth. Maybe wearing a mouth guard for hockey all these years has been like orthodonture. I could have saved my parents a whole lot of money if I had been a hockey player.

"After school. The equipment room. Don't be late."

And he was gone. The rest of the day was a blur. For some unknown cosmic reason, Chuck's attention had once more settled on me and he needed to hurt me. Then I'd have to walk, or probably limp home three miles. And I'd have to explain to Mom why I looked like what I'd look like.

Sam was waiting by my locker after the last class, as

usual. But from the way he was looking at me—and probably how I was looking back—we knew it wasn't a usual day. I grabbed my stuff. I had no idea what homework I had for the night or if I even had any. I took all my books. It might be a while before I could come back to school again, I reasoned.

"Well," I said. "I'll see you later." Over the weekend, I had convinced Sam and Mary not to come with me. It hadn't been easy. I had to tell them—and I really meant it—that I would never speak to them again if they did. I might be a retard to Chuck, but I didn't want to look like a retard who brought his retard friends along to get a beating too.

Sam clutched my arm. "There's still time! Don't be crazy! Get on the bus. He'll kill you."

"If not today, tomorrow. And besides, if I don't go, he'll be even madder, and you know what that means."

"I'm coming with you." Sam has the muscle tone of linguine. Chuck could take him out in, say, three seconds.

I sighed. "We've already been through this. No way. Get on the bus." My legs were rubbery and my whole body felt kind of shaky, but I wanted to get it over with. "Go!" My voice had been a little on the squeaky side, but I managed to make the last word sound forceful.

"I'll wait for you in front of the school. We'll walk home together."

I nodded and couldn't help giving a little groan. Sam knew what I was thinking. We'd walk home together if I could still walk.

The equipment storage room was filled with stacks of mats and metal shelves holding balls, bats—many instruments of torture. It didn't have any windows and it was at the end of a corridor away from everything else. Chuck was waiting for me outside. He opened the door and pushed me in. "Took you long enough, asshole."

I went flying and skidded across the concrete floor, ending up against one of the piles of mats. He pulled the door shut and locked it. There was only one light and it was dim. I closed my eyes and prayed that I wouldn't cry. I could already feel his fists pounding my face, my chest, my entire body. I hoped he wouldn't break anything. He'd broken Kevin Hart's nose a few years ago. Kevin told his parents he fell down the stairs running for his bus and they made a big stink about putting in carpeting or rubber treads to prevent injury. On top of the pain, he had to feel embarrassed about his parents.

I tried to think what I would tell *my* parents. My dad would think it was okay that I was in a fight—just not that I lost. He taught me how to throw a punch and wanted to get me some gloves when I was younger. He said every boy needed to know how to defend himself. I was pretty good at it and he was happy, but the gloves never appeared. Gloves with steel linings wouldn't help me now.

"Stand up, you moron." Chuck was grinning. Mom was right. He was really getting off on all this. He was feeling powerful—he *was* powerful.

I got up, but I felt really dizzy and didn't know whether my legs would support me. The room stank—a kind of musty smell from the mats, the equipment, a gym sock smell and something else. Something funky.

Chuck's grin got wider. "You take pills, right?"

Was that what he was going to get me for? For being in Club Meds, even if he didn't know it existed?

"Not pills, really." I was choking. "Medication."

He grabbed my shirt. "You take Ritalin. I know you do. You've been taking it since you were in third grade."

I was amazed that he'd been following the course of my treatment so thoroughly, and also felt further in the dark.

"Yeah, I take Ritalin."

"Well, you're going to be taking a lot less now." He

relaxed his grip and I sat down—hard. What the hell was he getting at? My heart was beating so fast, my chest hurt and I was having trouble getting a breath.

He sat next to me and took a candy bar from his knapsack. He didn't offer me a bite.

"Every Friday, you meet me here. Same time. I want two hundred milligrams. Twenty little white pills. For the weekend. That should do me to start."

"What! I can't do that!"

He got me in a hammerlock. "I don't want to hear that," he shouted. "It could make me mad." He loosened his hold and took another bite of his candy. It was a Snickers bar.

I tried to think. My head was spinning, and not just from the position he'd had it in. I begged. I knew it was pathetic, but it was the only thing I could do.

"Please—I can't give you my medication. The nurse keeps it locked up here and my mom would definitely notice if some was missing at home. She keeps very careful track."

Good old Mom. I would never yell at her again for being such a nag.

Chuck pulled his knapsack toward him. I thought he was going for another candy bar. Instead, he pulled out some breath mints. They weren't Tic Tacs, but some other kind in a flat, plastic container. He shook some out into the palm of his huge hand. They nestled there in the folds of fat and muscle. They looked like little white pills. They looked exactly like 10-milligram tablets of Ritalin.

"You must think I'm stupid or something. We wouldn't want your mother to fuck things up, now would we? You put back some of these. Hey, I'll even give you some to start." He thrust the container of mints into my hand and rubbed my hair in what would have been a friendly gesture with anyone else, but felt like it was being torn from its roots since this was Chuck.

Before I could stop myself I said the words that were screaming in my head out loud: "But, Chuck, if I replace my pills with this stuff, I won't have enough medication!"

He began to laugh so hard, he rolled around on the floor. I've only seen people do this in the movies. It was scary up close and not funny at all. I was feeling clammy and if I didn't get out of the room soon, I'd probably throw up.

I hadn't been off my meds since the day they were prescribed. Some kids don't take them in the summer or on weekends, but that didn't make any sense to me. If I need meds, I need meds all the time, not just for school. My doctor totally agrees and said he never could understand medication vacations— how was being cranky and out of control a pleasant vacation? But Mary says some kids like the feeling and some others refuse to take them to jerk their parents around. But I myself have never tried going without those little pills and I don't want to. Just thinking about it got me so frightened, I couldn't help it; I was going to cry. I closed my eyes. There wasn't much light in the room, but it was bright orange behind my lids. Hot tears began to seep out. I opened my eyes quick and blinked.

" 'Fraid you're going to flip out? 'Fraid you're going to do some psycho thing?" Chuck jeered. He got up and pretended to be Frankenstein's monster, stumbling around the room with his arms stretched out in front of him. I headed for the door. He got there first, opened it, and said, "Friday. Twenty pills or you're dead meat."

I wasn't surprised to see some of his friends standing around in the hall. They didn't even look at me. I was glad, because I was starting to cry for real. I went to the locker room and splashed my face with cold water, then took a pee. Pee the pain out. I fell off my bike when we were visiting my dad's sister once, and that's what she told me to do. It didn't help then and it didn't help now.

Sam was waiting. I knew he would be. Mary had a music lesson or she would have been there too.

"What happened? You don't look bad at all! Did he do it where nobody could see?"

He had, but not in the way Sam meant. I shook my head. "He didn't beat me up."

"He didn't beat you up! Then what did he want?" Sam looked astonished.

"Let's get going. I'll tell you on the way."

The truth was, I was still in shock. It was Monday. I had to come up with some kind of plan or give him the pills by the end of the week.

Deep down I knew I'd be giving him the pills.

chapter fifteen
CLUELESS

Sam waited for me to speak. He's really good at knowing the kind of mood I'm in.

After a while I told him. "Chuck wants my meds. I have to give him two hundred milligrams of Ritalin every Friday."

Sam stopped dead in his tracks. We were on the shortcut through the conservation land. We hadn't had the first frost yet, but a lot of the leaves were off the trees because of some hurricanes in Florida that turned into giant windstorms here. It looked pretty barren, not like the rest of the year when we liked to ride our bikes on the paths.

"You've got to be kidding! What would he want your Rits for? He's not ADHD. But wait a minute, I'm being really stupid. Of course he does. I'm surprised he hasn't been after you before this."

I'd worked it out for myself, too, in the few seconds after Chuck put it to me. Ritalin is speed. Ritalin is a drug. Kids like Chuck take drugs or sell drugs or take and sell drugs. I'd heard of kids taking Ritalin with alcohol to get high. On the pill containers there's a warning not to mix them with alcohol. I know I can't drink, but it's not something that has ever attracted me that much, so I've never felt deprived. Maybe I'll start to want a beer or some wine when I'm older. Maybe it will be hard not to, but I've always figured it's something I've got to live with. Like Joseph and his wheelchair, and when I think of that, I feel like not taking a drink is definitely no big deal.

Sam was jumping up and down the way he does when he gets excited. "I've heard that Chuck was dealing and now we've got the proof!"

"The proof to do what exactly?" I asked sarcastically. Sam wasn't thinking this thing through. True, I'd had more time to run every single possible scenario through my head like a million coming attractions and he hadn't, but any idiot could see where Sam's line of reasoning would end up for us.

Sam stopped his yo-yo imitation and said soberly, "We can't turn him in."

"No," I said, "we can't. Number one, he'd kill us, and number two, his friends would kill us."

"So what are we going to do?" It was nice of Sam to say "we."

"I haven't got a clue," I answered—and I didn't. We walked the rest of the way home without saying another word. Sam knew I didn't feel like talking. Mom calls it shutting down. I call it not talking.

As soon as I opened the kitchen door, my mother started in on me. Of course she was a crazy woman because I hadn't called to tell her I'd missed the bus. The champion worrier. The champion worrier who can't seem to get it through her head that I'm in *high school* now. Still, I wanted to blurt the whole thing out to her, that calling her was the last thing on my mind after Chuck let me go, and by the way, could she please take care of this whole mess? But I apologized and didn't even complain when she unplugged my keyboard and took away my computer privileges for some unspecified time.

"You have *got* to understand how serious this is. I was just about to call the police. I called the school and they paged you. There was no answer. Then I called Sam's mother and he wasn't home either, so we figured that it wasn't likely that both of you had been kidnapped or run over, but you can't do this again, Jack. It's not fair to me."

This is one of Mom's favorite lines and when I'm really fighting with her, I'll say what about being fair to me? But today was not one of those days. In fact, I was so unresponsive that she put her hand on my forehead and wanted to know if I felt sick. I felt sick, all right, but it was nothing that a thermometer could measure. For a moment, I thought about staying home for the rest of the week, but I'd have to go back to school sometime and Chuck would be waiting. Extremely pissed off and waiting.

She gave me my pills and told me to start my homework. I always have to do it right after school so I get done before supper. After supper I'm coming off my meds. I get really tired, but I'd never let Mom know. I began to think of how I feel during the time when the Ritalin has pretty much worn off and I haven't taken the nighttime pills before getting into bed. Chuck didn't know about these pills or I'd have to be forking them over too. I have no doubt he knows a substitute look-alike for every drug he wants to abuse or push. Anyway, I decided to take only 10 milligrams of my after-school meds—half—

and see what happened. I put the other pill in an envelope and stuck it in my top desk drawer. Only nineteen more to go.

The worst thing about Chuck's plan was that it was a good one. It was as if he'd slipped into my house and seen the whole setup. Mom keeps all my meds on a shelf in one of the kitchen cupboards. We get a month's supply at a time. There was a smaller container with yellow 5-milligram pills, and if I was going to be up late, like going to the movies with one of my friends or something, she'd give me a little extra. The larger container has the white 10-milligram size, and she would never notice that the breath mints didn't have the number or letters on them and weren't scored the way Ritalin is. If she's not home, I get them myself, but usually she shakes out the pills—two in the morning, two in the late afternoon—puts them in my hand, and closes the container up. I pop them in my mouth right away.

This was another creepy thing about Chuck's plan. It was like he'd been watching us through a window and knew I'd have to have substitute pills to put in the container. I couldn't just palm my Rits to give to him. I'd have to have two pills to take right there in front of

Mom. Afterward, only I would know by the taste whether I was going to have fresh breath and a blank brain or the opposite, at least the brain part. I know Ritalin helps me focus my thoughts. It's like putting a car into drive. Without it, I'd be stuck in neutral—or worse, reverse.

I sat down at the kitchen table and started my math. It was going okay. An hour later, I picked up the book we're doing in English, *The Pearl,* by John Steinbeck. I read a couple of pages, then realized I had no idea what I'd read. I went back and started again. I began to get this very panicky feeling, but I didn't want Mom to know anything was wrong. Wasn't it too soon for the meds to be wearing off? But I'd had only half a dose. The words on the page seemed to be connected in long lines across the page with no spaces in between, unless I said them out loud in my head. I closed the book, got up, and was super casual. "Well, that's it for today. Mind if I call Sam? See if we can maybe go to the Museum of Science or something next weekend."

"Great, honey. Go right ahead. Dad will be home for dinner. His plane landed at four."

I went to the den and took the portable phone up to my room. One thing about telling lies. Once you start, it gets easier and easier. I wasn't calling Sam. I was calling Mary.

Mary makes Mom nervous. "It isn't that I don't like her; it's just that when you're together, you don't seem like my Jack." I still don't know what this means, but what really upsets Mom about Mary is that she is a girl—a teenage girl. We weren't allowed to be in my room alone together, although I've pointed out to Mom that if Mary and I wanted to fool around, we could do it anywhere, especially since our town has acres of woods. That seemed to upset Mom even more, so I keep Mom and Mary separate and slip over to her house instead. Her parents both work full-time. Her older brother, who is supposed to keep an eye on things, is usually in the basement, where he has a darkroom, and Mary's little sister goes to extended daycare. I'd hang out at Mary's more, but most days I have homework and then there's Mom. . . .

I told Mary that Chuck hadn't beaten me up, but there was still a big problem. She said to come over right away and not say anything more on the phone if I was on a portable. She saw this on *60 Minutes* or something—how anybody can tap in and hear what you say on a portable. I told Mom I was going for a bike ride. See what I mean? Lies, lies. I mean, yes, I *was* going for a bike ride, but no, I wasn't really going for a bike ride.

Mary was sitting on her back porch. She had a bright red down vest on and her cheeks were just as red. She looked excited. "What's going on? You don't look hurt, but you look terrible."

"Thanks a lot." I was in a rotten mood. I should've taken both pills. Dad would be at dinner and he'd be tired from the trip. I saw an old movie once where this lady said, "Fasten your seat belts, it's going to be a bumpy night." That was the way I was feeling.

"Come on." Mary moved over, reached in her pocket, and took out a Butterfinger. She knows how much I love Butterfingers. No comparison to Snickers bars.

"Chuck says I have to give him some of my meds every Friday. He gave me these to replace them so my parents won't find out." I took the container of mints from my pocket and handed it to her.

"What an asshole." Mary was furious. "If I were his mother or father, I'd be seriously worried. He's the type who'd replace their nitro tablets with sugar pills at their deathbeds and be laughing while they're dying of heart attacks."

Mary watches *ER* and picked up a big, fat, red reference book called *Physicians' Desk Reference* at a library book sale once. She'd flipped through it and saw that it listed every prescription drug, describing it and its possible side effects. It even had pictures of the pills. It was out of date, but not by much. We spend hours looking stuff up and have the Ritalin section almost memorized.

Mary was ticking off things on her fingers. "Obviously we can't go to the Phantom or the Mad Scheduler. Even if they were normal administrators, we'd never make it to graduation—no, make that the end of next week."

There was that nice "we" thing again. Like with Sam. My heart began to slow down for the first time since my rendezvous with Chuck. *Rendezvous.* Maybe I remember more French than I think. *Guillotine.* That's another. I tuned back into Mary, really wishing I had taken both after-school pills. My mind was surfing.

Mary was still listing possibilities. She pointed to another finger. "Parents—definitely out. We could never convince your mother to do anything but blow the whistle big-time on Chuck, and your dad the same. Of course he might go ballistic and find it necessary to hurt Chuck, which would be nice."

We both contemplated the pleasant thought for a moment—Chuck with shiners, Chuck with missing teeth, Chuck in a cast. "But the same thing would happen. Chuck would get into deep shit now, but you'd be a marked man for the rest of your days in school—no, make that in the whole town."

Mary wasn't really helping much. There were all those "make that"s. My heart began to pick up speed.

She ticked off another finger. "Police out, same reason, which leaves teachers. I can think of one or two we could go to, like Ms. Anderson or Mr. Greenberg. They're at least semisane." Mary is very judgmental, so "semisane" was high praise. In fact, both of these teachers were great. "But I think there's some kind of law that says they have to tell something like this. Even if they wanted to try to help us figure out a way to stop Chuck without his knowing you squealed, they couldn't."

Unfortunately, I was pretty sure she was right. In any case, even the best teachers will tell you what you say will be held in strictest confidence, but somehow it still gets out.

Mary frowned. "This is going to take some thought.

You may have to give him the pills this week. I'll give you ten of mine before you leave just in case, and you give me ten of those mints."

I started to protest, but she wouldn't let me get a word out. "We're in this together, Jack. He's not going to stop with you. You're the trial run—or maybe he's already doing it to other kids. Eventually he's going to be on to every kid who's taking any medication he can get high on or sell. He's going to concentrate on the older kids, 'cause the younger ones might crack and tell their parents or a teacher. Maybe that's why he left your meds alone when he was in middle school. No matter what, we've got to do something. Chuck the Puck's got to be stopped." She stood up. "We can do it. Club Meds can do it."

She reminded me of Joan of Arc. I just hoped Chuck didn't carry matches.

I got home barely in time for dinner. Dad was in a bad mood. Maybe the deal he'd been working on had fallen through. Maybe there hadn't been any peanuts on his flight. Whatever the reason, I prayed we could get through the meal without me being sent from the table. I concentrated on my chewing. Nobody was talking.

"We've been invited to the Jamesons' for dinner Saturday night. What should I tell them?" Mom said in a pretty good imitation of a cheerful voice. Mary is always talking about women's intuition and how girls are more plugged in to the way people think and act than boys. Maybe it's true, but tonight, Mom's ESP was experiencing a power failure. Even I knew that the last thing Dad was interested in talking about was going to somebody's house on the weekend.

"Tell them what they called 'dinner' was so bad last time that we'll only come if we can bring our own. Tell them . . . tell them anything you want." He pushed his plate away. He hadn't eaten much, even though Mom had roasted a chicken and made her special garlic mashed potatoes, food he usually inhales in one gulp.

Mom pressed her lips together. Never a good sign.

It was my turn.

"So how's school, champ?" Dad asked. "Champ." That wasn't a good sign either.

I didn't say anything. A few seconds dragged by.

"I asked you a question and I expect an answer."

"Robert." Mom gave him the look, but he was staring at me.

"You want me to be interested in what he's doing

and I'm interested. How is school?" He spoke slowly, exaggerating each word.

Even when I'm on my meds, at times like this I can't think. It's like my mind is too full and too empty at once. You're probably wondering why I couldn't just say "fine" or something else marginally dumb, but at least it would have been an answer. I *wanted* to, but I couldn't find the word. Finally I found the words that I can always pull out of the hat.

"I don't know."

"You don't know how school is? You go there every day and spend what, six, seven hours there, and you don't know?" Dad was still talking in that slow way.

"Robert, leave him alone," Mom cried out.

He turned and looked at her. "Fine, Diane. I'll leave him alone. I'll leave you both alone."

He went into the den and turned on the TV.

"I'm sorry," I whispered.

"It's not your fault," Mom snapped. She had two red spots on her cheeks, but they were different from Mary's.

I helped her clear the table and put the food away. When she went down to the basement to put a wash in, I took nine pills from the container and put nine mints in, trying to mix them around below the top layer, but Mom was coming back, so I don't think I did a great job. I figured I might as well just do it. Ten from Mary and now ten from me. Done.

Then I went to my room and lay down on my bed. Great, I thought. Chuck is shaking me down for my meds, and my parents are on the brink of a divorce because of me. I was trying to feel pissed at them all, but kept feeling sad instead. Mom knocked on the door, saw me on the bed, and felt my forehead again. She gave this big sigh, handed me the night pills, and said, "Get some sleep; you look tired. Your father's tired too; don't worry. Everything will be fine tomorrow."

See what I mean about women's intuition? To be blunt, sometimes it sucks.

Tuesday and Wednesday Mary, Sam, and I tried to think of a way I could get out of giving Chuck my meds. By Thursday, I didn't want to discuss it anymore. I was going to give them to him and that was that. I'd worry about next week, next week.

Having a plan, even if the plan was to give Chuck the pills, made it possible to get through the day. It also helped that I didn't run in to him. But Friday, as soon as I got off my bus, he was waiting with his arms folded across his chest. He was wearing one of those team jackets, and his muscles puffed out every inch of it. I realized I was staring at him, wondering what he was going to look like by his senior year if he kept growing and working out the way he did. I wanted to think of him as a cartoon character or action figure, something not real, but there he was in the flesh—a lot of it—blocking my way to homeroom.

"See you after school. You got something for me?"

I nodded.

"Gooood." He smirked and jabbed me as I walked past him up the stairs. It felt like a booster shot, where your arm aches for a week.

I had a history test and a quiz in math. I think I did okay, but I never know how I do on these things, even when I'm on full meds. I'd taken one and one again before school—a mint and a med. Some days I'd been lucky; some days not. I was feeling kind of annoyed with the world, but who wouldn't be in my situation? There had been more times than usual that I hadn't realized that I was supposed to be listening to someone and answering back. But none of that mattered. I had the twenty pills.

The only problem was that Mary and Sam were

giving me so many knowing, sympathetic looks that I swear even the teachers could have picked up on them. Kids were looking at me in a puzzled way, and the whole ninth grade knew something was going on.

After school I went straight to the equipment room. I wanted to get it over with. Chuck was waiting. He put his hand out. I gave him the envelope and turned to leave.

"Not so fast, faggot." He didn't have to lay a hand on me. I stopped.

He ripped open the envelope and counted the pills, examining each one to make sure I hadn't slipped a mint in. I wanted to tell him I didn't have a death wish and he could trust me, but Chuck doesn't trust anyone.

"See you next week. Same time, same place. Oh, and have a good weekend. I know I will." He transferred the Ritalin into a film canister and put it in his knapsack.

I wanted to kill him. Instead, I walked down the hall, up the stairs, and right past my locker, not even noticing that Mary and Sam were waiting there for me.

"Jack!" Mary called. "Get you stuff and call your mother. Tell her you're going to the center for ice cream with some kids." Mary knew Mom wasn't crazy about her. Mary didn't take it personally, though. She'd told me, "Look, it's not like we're girlfriend and boyfriend, but that's what's in the back of your mom's head. And aside from not wanting to lose her baby boy to another woman, the idea of you ending up with someone who's on meds too has got to make her nervous. Clueless and clueless—not your mom's ideal match."

I'd never thought of this, but it made sense. In her own way, Mary usually did. She says a lot of it comes from reading the magazine *Jane*.

Mom gave me permission, reminding me to stop at the nurse's office for the after-school meds Mom would have given me. I knew she wouldn't object. It was the old friendship-pool strategy. In her head, I was on my way to the malt shop with all the class officers, my new best friends.

"Okay, that's done. Now we *have* to come up with a plan. Look, we've got a whole week more." Mary tried to make it sound like a long time. Even I realized it was no time at all.

Joseph was at Friendly's, sitting in the parking lot by the take-out window drinking hot chocolate. It was kind of nippy for ice cream.

"I asked Joseph to meet us here," Sam said as we walked over. "He lives near Chuck, and besides, he's smart."

I had no problem with it. I don't know what kind of medication Joseph got from the nurse every day. It had never come up, but if it was an upper, downer, or in-betweener, Chuck would want it. Besides, the more, the merrier, since I still couldn't see a way out. For the last five days I'd been trying to come to terms with the fact that, without my meds, I'd be as messed up as the kids who were abusing them. Only in a different way.

"I thought we should include Joseph, but nobody else. It's not safe. We know we won't tell anybody, but the more people who know, the greater the risk," Sam said in this serious way he has. It sounded very professional and reassuring—like, "Your tumor can be removed."

I nodded and then said, "By the way, stop giving me all those sick puppy dog looks in the halls. That's bound to start rumors, if they haven't started already."

Mary and Sam looked guilty. I guess they hadn't realized what they were doing.

"We're wasting time. Let's order and go sit in the playground. There won't be anybody there at this time of year," Mary said.

Parents in town had raised money for this huge playground with all sorts of neat stuff—bridges to cross, tunnels, and lots of tire swings, which all kids love. I remember when my mom said I was too old to go there anymore. It was a big shock. I had never thought I'd be too old for anything.

We sat down next to Joseph under one of the huge pine trees not far from the slides.

An hour later, we were exactly where we'd started.

"I have to go," Sam said. "Why don't we sleep on it and meet tomorrow? Maybe a solution will appear to us in a dream."

"I can make it; in fact, come to my house," Joseph said. "And I'll think really hard tonight. There's got to be a way we can expose Chuck without his knowing it was us—or without Jack getting into trouble too."

"What are you talking about?" I asked. This was something new. How could I get in trouble? I was the victim!

"Well," he explained to me, "we all know Chuck is not a nice guy. If he gets caught, he's going to try to get out of it any way he can. Probably the first thing he'd do is say you're dealing and sold him the pills, and it was all your fault."

I hadn't thought things could get any worse, but they just had.

chapter sixteen
COMIC RELIEF

I almost forgot to write about a funny thing that happened this week. Maybe not so funny at the time. No, definitely funny at the time.

Wednesday morning my homeroom teacher told me my guidance counselor wanted to see me. I said I'd make an appointment, but she said my counselor wanted to see me right away, and gave me a pass. This was weird. I'd met with Mr. Hill at the very beginning of the year and we'd had a thirty-second conversation about goals. I'd passed him in the halls a few times, but that doesn't count.

I began to bite my thumbnail. I've never been a nail biter. Now seemed like a good time to start. Why did Mr. Hill want to see me? Could I have been totally wrong and in fact the administration *did* know what Chuck was up to? But then it would be Mr. Dolan, the vice principal, the scheduling maniac, who would be calling me into his office. He was in charge of discipline, which gives you a good idea why the Chucks of the school were doing so well.

I told the guidance secretary who I was and took a seat. It was one of those molded plastic ones that look like the bowl of a spoon and part of the handle. Extremely uncomfortable. I was just beginning to wonder why none of the furniture in schools is ever comfortable—I mean is it to punish kids? Keep them alert and in pain, or what?—when I saw something that really scared the shit out of me. Worse than anything I had imagined walking down here. Something out of a nightmare. It was my mother's coat.

I knew it was hers because it still had the WALK FOR HUNGER button on it from last spring. I also knew it was hers because the pocket was just a tiny bit ripped and she's been saying for weeks that she has to sew it up. Now what are the odds that someone in the guidance department or visiting the guidance department would have hung up a coat exactly the same color and style with the same button and same rip? Lousy, but I was praying for a long shot.

Mr. Hill opened his office door. "Oh good, Jack, you're here. Come in."

Mom's face was all crumpled up and she was holding a tissue. I'd had a knot in my stomach in the waiting room. It was a whole ball of twine now.

Things got even stranger. Mr. Margolis was there. Again, what are the odds? Out of all the teachers in the school, my *Wellness* teacher has figured out something's going on? Then it came to me in a flash. Something must have happened to make Chuck think he was going to be found out and he went to his trusted jock teacher pal and said I'd approached him about buying drugs or a similar lie. Mr. Margolis works out a lot and definitely favors Chuck and his friends. One day after school when they were trying to stuff Sam in a locker, and he was walking by, he just told them to stop horsing around.

I looked at Mr. Hill's gray metal wastebasket and thought I would puke.

Then I looked at what was on his desk and the relief was so great, I thought I'd puke anyway.

"Now, Jack, Mr. Margolis brought your last Life Skills quiz to our attention and we're a little concerned about the way you answered some of the questions."

Some of the questions? How about all of the questions? It was the one I got an "F" on. We each have a folder he keeps in the room for all our corrected stuff. I think he knows we'd toss it and we're supposed to hold on to these for life, in case we ever have some sort of values problem that a drawing of a tree will help solve.

"Jack," Mom said in a shaky voice, "have you been upset about something lately? Have you been feeling depressed?"

Upset? Depressed? I looked around the room at everybody. I was definitely outnumbered. This is something adults are really good at—outnumbering kids. It gives them an automatic advantage. Normally I am not claustrophobic—just mention "spelunking" to Sam and he has to open a window—but I was feeling a real lack of air. I took a deep breath. They were all staring at me.

"No." Well, I wasn't—not in the way they were thinking. And this is when it started to get funny. A minute earlier I was afraid I was going to puke; now I was afraid I was going to laugh. It was a quiz, a stupid little quiz! Even if it had ever been a possibility, this wasn't going to put the Ivy League out of my reach. There would be plenty of big things like finals, papers, SATs, my whole GPA looming ahead for that.

Mr. Margolis put a hand on my shoulder. It was as heavy as Chuck's.

"Maybe you could tell us what you were thinking about when you answered the way you did?" He sounded super sympathetic.

"I wasn't thinking anything. I mean, I couldn't think of anything," I tried to explain.

Mr. Hill looked a little exasperated. I began to see the whole picture. Mr. Margolis handed me back the quiz with an "F," then maybe he saw something on TV about depressed teens or somebody said something in the teachers' room that made him think he ought to cover his butt and let my counselor know I had written the word "dead" on a Life Skills quiz. I mean, I'm sure Mr. Margolis thought I was being a wise ass, but what if they found me hanging in the attic with a note with the quiz questions in my pocket? In his mind, and obviously Mr. Hill's, there were only two choices: depression or acting out. Mr. Hill was now very obviously leaning toward "kid is a jerk."

I had one last hope. Mom. Mr. Margolis sat down and I looked at my mother.

"I don't even know what I'll be like at the end of ninth grade. I assume I'll be here," I said, although the way things were looking lately, maybe that was a false assumption, but I kept going. "That is, I'll be finishing freshman year, but ten years from now? Twenty years, *fifty* years?" My voice got pretty high-pitched.

"The point of the exercise is to help you define your goals and sharpen your future perspective," Mr. Hill said sternly.

Mom came through. She tucked her Kleenex in her pocket and straightened her skirt.

"Kids with ADHD have a lot of trouble anticipating the future. They tend to live in the moment, and for Jack, next week can seem as far away as Christmas. Sometimes I wish I was a little ADHD myself and didn't worry so much about the future."

The two men exchanged glances. They'd heard this bullshit before, was what I picked up. Mom flushed. She was used to it too—that she was covering for me and using ADHD as an excuse. She stood up. "I have to be leaving now, and Jack is missing English." Mom knows my schedule better than I do. "Thank you for being so concerned, and perhaps on future quizzes if Jack has a problem, he can speak to you about it, Mr. Margolis?"

"Sure, sure." Mr. Margolis seemed anxious to get back to the gym. I'd be, too, if I were wearing shorts, a T-shirt, and a whistle around my neck. He'd done what he thought he was supposed to do, and hey—no sweat.

Mr. Hill walked us out and helped my mother on with her coat.

"We'll talk some more when you get home," she said, and kissed me. I hate when she does that—both things.

On the way back to class, I kept trying not to laugh. I was smiling so hard that anyone passing would have thought I was a lunatic. Irony. That's what it was. Something straight out of an English teacher's lecture, except not boring. I mean, I have a gigantic problem and end up in a heavy duty meeting at guidance over something like this. Irony. Ironic.

I like walking through the halls when they're empty. I figured I could take a minute or two more before going back to class, but not much more than that. Teachers have calculated down to the last second how long it takes to get from anywhere in the building to their own particular classroom. But I couldn't help myself. It was such a good feeling, walking alone. All the classroom doors have windows, but most teachers covered these up with posters. I guess the idea is so kids won't be distracted by other kids passing by. They couldn't see out, and I couldn't see in. I could almost make myself believe that I was alone in the building. That there'd been a nuclear war and I was the only person left.

It was real quiet. My shoes made a soft, shuffling sound, but that was it. I walked by the empty cafeteria. There was a kind of stale pizza smell mixed with a stale baloney sandwich smell. Mary says I have an abnormally sensitive sense of smell. Napoleon did too. She did a paper on him for history last year and found out a lot of extremely interesting things. He could make himself go to sleep for any amount of time too. Like he'd be about to go into battle and he'd say, "I'm going to nap for ten minutes," then ten minutes later there he was jumping up on his horse.

Anyway, all the schools I've ever been in smell the same. The cleaning stuff the custodians use for the floors and bathrooms, grungy clothes kids have left in their lockers too long, spearmint gum, rubber—I don't know what makes that smell, a whifty hint of vomit, and that day as I was roaming around smiling, panic. It was pushing its way back up to the surface. Chuck was going to be wanting his pills—*my pills*—in a few days. There was nothing comic about it—and no relief in sight.

chapter seventeen

BRAINSTORMING

We were sitting in Joseph's room. I always like going over to his house—good eats, and his mother doesn't keep popping her head in the door to see if anyone wants something. She assumes if we do, we'll get it, which we had. An empty bag of Doritos and an almost empty jar of salsa were on the floor. We were working on a big bottle of Coke. Joseph's room is filled with signed baseballs and basketballs, posters of players, all kinds of jock stuff, but it went with the kid and never put me off. To be truthful, I thought it was kind of cool and wished I could get more interested in sports myself. Watching them, that is.

Last night I'd had what seemed like a brilliant idea at the time. I wasn't going to take any more meds from Mary, plus I really needed to be getting my full dose. If I took twenty out and put twenty mints at the very bottom,

I'd be all set. By the time I got that low, maybe we'd have figured out something to do.

Mom and Dad were watching *Mystery!* on PBS. When I walked by the den and looked in, they were holding hands. I don't know whether it was from fear or love, but it made me feel good. I went into the kitchen and poured myself a glass of milk and opened the cabinet where my pills are. I had the mints in the envelope in my pocket. I dumped the pills on the counter. The show lasted an hour, but you can't count on adults to stay focused that long. One or the other was bound to come out to the kitchen for a snack or to go to the bathroom, which was next to the pantry. I counted out twenty pills, put the mints in the bottom, filled the container with the rest of the pills, and screwed the child-proof cap back on. I'd just put the envelope in my pocket when Mom's voice caught me totally by surprise and I knocked the bottle off the counter. It rolled along the kitchen floor and came to a stop by her foot.

"What are you doing up, Jack? I gave you your stoppers." She picked up the container. "This is your Ritalin. What's going on?"

"I was just checking to see that I had enough for the rest of the month," I stammered.

"This isn't like you. You've never worried about your medication before. Maybe you need to be checked again. You may not be getting enough. Do you feel undermedicated?"

There was that question again. I *never* know when I need more. Until now, that is. I think Mom gauges it by how fast I'm growing and how much milk she buys rather than my behavior, but she doesn't always tell me everything. I felt a flicker of hope. If the doctor upped my dosage, I'd have more to give away. But a little voice said, if you really need more, nothing will change. You'll still be screwed.

"I'll make an appointment. It's been a while. You should be seen, anyway." She put the pills back in the cabinet. "Get some sleep, sweetheart. Good night."

"Good night, Mom." I gave her a hug. It wasn't her fault.

I was back where I'd started from.

Sure enough, the bottle rolling around on the floor had destroyed my careful arrangement. I'd left for Joseph's this morning with minty clean breath. One of the meds Mom had automatically doled out was a dud. The damn mints really did look like the pills. Somebody would have had to point out the difference to Mom, and that somebody sure as hell wasn't going to be me.

From now on, it was going to be like playing Russian roulette. I couldn't examine the pills before I put them in my mouth, so I was going to have to do the tongue test to figure out what I was getting. Ritalin tastes very gross, which is why I always just swallow it. Mary is sure it gives people bad breath and she's switched from Tic Tacs to the brand of mints Chuck gave me. She likes it that they look the same. Don't ask me why.

I'm not sure if it was the low dose or just my life right now, but I was getting pretty anxious. I didn't want to tell everybody the stupid thing I'd done. Before I went to sleep, I'd felt pretty hopeless. Even if it had worked, we were never going to come up with a plan—which meant a future of "dates" with Chuck on Friday afternoons. Even if I hadn't dropped the pills, I would have had twenty mints instead of Ritalin in the future and how would I have gotten around that problem? Mints for every dose.

"Let's get organized." Obviously this wasn't Mary or me. It was Sam. He had a pad of paper and a pencil. "Jack's down ten pills, so's Mary"—I almost corrected him, make that thirty for me, since I'd taken the twenty out, but I didn't, getting stuck instead on how big a number it was—"and we can't let another week go by. We have to approach the problem scientifically. What do we know about Chuck? What are his likes, dislikes?"

I couldn't really see where this was going to get us, but anything was worth a shot, at this point.

Joseph's face lit up. I must have missed something. "Okay, profile of the bully. The way cops do a profile of a criminal. Great idea. Likes are easy. Sports, especially hockey."

"Maybe you could trade him season tickets to the Bruins in exchange for leaving you alone?" Mary offered.

"Oh, sure. I have them right here in my pocket—and even if you didn't have to put your name in practically when you're born to get them, it wouldn't stop Chuck from going after other kids."

"True, but I think we ought to say any and everything that comes into our heads," Mary said.

"You do that anyway." I was feeling like a grouch.

"Shut up." Mary smiled. "We know you're going nuts, you don't have to prove it."

"Okay, he likes sports." Sam was scribbling. "What else?"

"Drugs, alcohol, specifically Budweiser," Joseph listed. "I sometimes see the cans on Sunday mornings tossed in the bushes at the end of the street near where he and his friends hang out."

We sat thinking for a moment. I couldn't come up with anything else. The only activities Chuck had ever been involved with at school were related to sports. He was the class treasurer, though. You'd think someone like Chuck would never be elected to a position of such responsibility, but his friends all thought it would be a joke to nominate him and then a bigger joke to elect him.

"Money," I said. "He likes money."

Sam nodded and wrote.

"Sex," Mary said. "His eyeballs almost drop out when a good-looking girl goes by, and he's always had girlfriends. Not that I'm offering myself, you understand. I love you, Jack, but there are things no woman should ever have to do. Plus, it would probably destroy any chance I have to develop a normal, healthy sexual appetite. I'd never be able to look at another guy without being revolted just thinking about Chuck's—"

"We get it, we get it!" I yelled. "Nobody's asking you

to do anything remotely close to sleeping with him. *Capisce?*"

Mary was laughing. So were Sam and Joseph. I drank some Coke. My mom gets decaffeinated everything, even Coke, and I could feel the caffeine ricocheting in my brain, bouncing off the breath mint.

"Dislikes?" Sam asked.

"Us, school, teachers—although he sucks up a lot—us again, or make that everybody except his own group."

"Can we think of anything he'd be afraid of—anything that might put the fear of God in him?" Sam was getting into this profile thing.

"He's afraid of his father," Joseph said. "When he was a little kid, he'd even hide here if his old man was after him for doing something wrong—like losing a game. Mr. Williams has a wicked temper. You can hear him yelling at his kids, even when they're inside their house."

For a moment, I almost felt sorry for Chuck, then I remembered the way he'd slapped me around by my locker.

"If he got arrested for dealing, his father would freak. He'd be barred from team sports," Mary pointed out.

"So how do we get him arrested without getting

involved ourselves? Send an anonymous tip to the police? We'd still have to give my name and he'd know I squealed to someone." We'd been going down this same road for over a week now, and the ruts were up to my armpits.

"I have the feeling the solution is staring us in the face. It's like a mystery. We need Nancy Drew," Mary said.

"Yeah, I wish we had good old Nancy Drew around," Joseph kidded. "She'd know what to do."

"That's it!" Sam exclaimed.

"What are you talking about? Duh! For your information, Mr. Gold, Nancy Drew is fiction. Nancy Drew, girl detective. I still love those books," Mary said.

Sam gave her an "I know that, dummy" look and said, "Just hear me out. Think about everything we've listed about Chuck, what he likes, what he doesn't, what he's afraid of. We can use this—or somebody else can. We have to try to come up with someone who's not in school who can get something on Chuck and can't be traced back to us. Like in that old movie *The Sting*. Make Chuck think he's caught, only he really isn't, but he doesn't know that, so he stops."

Did I ever mention that my friend Sam is a fucking genius?

chapter eighteen

THE SOLUTION?

For a few minutes nobody said anything, even Mary. We were just thinking. I was biting my thumbnail, my new bad habit. Suddenly Mary jumped up and started to talk. "Sam, you're brilliant! I should have thought of this right away myself. It's foolproof. We get somebody—obviously a female—to come to school, get Chuck to fall for her—all she has to do is wave her hand around his crotch—and she finds out what he's doing because he's bound to brag about it. Of course she already knows, because we've told her. Then she turns on him and threatens to tell his father and the police if he doesn't cut it out!"

"Hold on, hold on." After listening to Mary, I wasn't sure Sam's idea was so inspired after all. "First of all, who are we going to get to come to school and pretend to be a member of our class? It would have to be someone in school somewhere else, and how would she explain to her parents and her own school why she was absent for however many days this would take? And don't you think Chuck, dumb as he is, would think it was a little fishy that this mystery woman arrives at school just when he's started hassling me, busts him, and then disappears? And what about all the teachers and Mr. Dolan? A girl suddenly shows up as a new student and they're not going to say something?"

"No, no, Mary's right! This can work. It *is* foolproof." Sam was really psyched. He was bouncing up and down on Joseph's bed. "She doesn't go to any classes, just lunch, and hangs out in the halls. The teachers, if they notice her, will assume she's in somebody else's class. If we went to a small school, it would be different, but Busby's a zoo. Same thing for the administrators. The Phantom, even if she did catch sight of her, would assume she's a student here. Think how long we've been here. Does Ms. McConnelly know your name or have any idea who you are?"

Sam was right. The principal posed no problem. "What about Mr. Dolan? He registers new students. He'd notice someone new."

"We tell whoever we get to stay away from the main

office as much as possible. Chuck never goes near it, and she's going to be where he is. If worse comes to worst and she does get caught, she can say she's visiting for the day. That she's going to be moving here. She can give some phony name."

"She can even say it was arranged by the Central Office." Mary's eyes were sparkling. "Like 'Didn't you get the call?'"

I had to laugh at that. Mr. Dolan had a running feud with the Central Office, where the superintendent was. Maybe they wanted him to do something besides scheduling—hard to say. One of Mary's friends worked in the main office at lunchtime when the secretaries had a break and she said Dolan was always muttering about "Central Office Directives."

Maybe I was as crazy as my friends. Maybe I was just very, very desperate, but the whole thing was beginning to make sense.

Except who?

"Okay, maybe this could work," I said, "but where are we going to find this girl—someone completely unknown to anyone in the school, our age, and willing to do it?"

She wouldn't actually be breaking any laws. Not

going to school was against the law, but I'd never heard of anything that said you could be arrested *for* going.

Sam had looked super serious before. Now he looked like one of those cartoons where the cat ate the canary—not Tweety, of course, some other bird.

"I've already thought of that. Kara. My cousin Kara. She's a sophomore at Boston University and I'm positive she'd help. In fact, this is just the kind of thing she gets off on. And she'd be perfect. Nobody knows her. She's never even been to the school. She has a car and can get here easily. And she's short—she can easily pass as a high school student. It shouldn't take more than a couple of days. I'll give her a call now. Since it's Saturday, she she won't be in class."

"Kara? Whoa, wait a minute, Sam. Didn't I meet her at the lake? There's no way she could pass for a ninth grader! She may be short, but she's, well, you know what I mean."

Sam's mother's family had been going to this lake in New Hampshire since the Cenozoic era and I've been up there with him a few times. I met Kara at the beginning of last summer. She was there with her boyfriend. True, she wasn't all that tall, but everything else about her was very mature. She has blond hair hanging straight to her shoulders, and that day she was wearing some kind of short summer dress that tied around her neck and didn't have much of a back. I didn't see any lines in her tan.

"Don't worry." Sam was reaching for Joseph's phone. "Haven't you ever heard of disguises? Actresses in the movies are always playing people much younger than they really are, and that's what Kara's going to be doing—acting."

I was still seeing Kara in that dress. Chuck would take the bait, all right, but I didn't like the idea of using her this way. What would happen if Chuck found out what she was doing? What would he do to her?

"No," I said firmly. "She could get hurt if Chuck figures out what's going on. We're not talking about some code of chivalry here (King Arthur, eighth-grade English). This is Chuck. He'd do something to her. You know he would."

Sam was still grinning. "First of all, Kara's not only taken self-defense classes, she's teaching them now. And second, you've met Max, her brother, right?"

I'd forgotten about Max. He wasn't just big; he was very big. And strong. It took him about three strokes to swim across the lake.

I gave in, or rather everybody was ignoring me and

talking at once about how cool the whole idea was. The Coke was gone. I went into the kitchen, found some more, and poured a tall glassful. Things were out of hand, but my whole life was, so it probably didn't matter how much caffeine I had.

When I came back into the room, everything was arranged. Kara was going to meet us at Mary's in an hour. This would be the one and only time we could get together, except to talk by phone or IM. We'd all have to pretend we didn't know her at school, and we certainly couldn't be seen with her outside the building. Mary's was the only house where nobody was home. I was feeling pretty keyed up—and I was sure it wasn't just the caffeine. The only thing I wanted everybody to understand was that we were going to tell Kara right away that if she didn't want to do it, she should say so and we'd figure something else out. Chivalry was *not* dead.

Mary, Sam, and I walked over to her house. Joseph was coming later. My watch beeped. I reached in my pocket for my meds. Mom had put them in a small Baggie.

"If any of them are mints, I'll give you some of mine when we get to my house," Mary offered.

I examined each pill carefully. One mint, the other

okay. I accepted her offer. I had the feeling I was going to need all my powers of concentration in the next few hours.

When Kara walked onto the porch, I didn't recognize her. Her hair was pulled back in a ponytail, and the only makeup she had on was something shiny and pink on her lips. She was wearing jeans and a light blue T-shirt under a big, khaki army surplus jacket. She looked like a kid.

She was laughing. "What's the matter, Jack? Don't you recognize me?"

I could feel myself blush. "Sure, I mean, not really," I stammered.

"Perfect," Mary said admiringly, "you'll blend right in. None of the adults will look twice at you, but all the guys will." Inside the house, Kara had taken off her jacket. Her T-shirt wasn't tight enough to be slutty, but hugged her body in the right places. Chuck has all the luck, I found myself thinking, before I remembered this was not going to be one of his lucky times—not if we could pull this off.

"Okay, so tell me about this creep. Everything. I have to get the whole picture."

We filled her in and she wrinkled her nose in disgust. I realized again what we were asking her to do, and there was no way I was going through with it. Forget the meds. Forget me. We were asking another human being to prostitute herself, and I felt kind of sick.

"It's off. The whole thing is off," I heard myself say. "You're not doing it."

Kara gave me a funny look. I couldn't tell whether she agreed or disagreed. It sort of seemed like she was proud of me, which was hard for me to believe. "Take a walk in the backyard with me, Jack. We need to talk."

I wasn't going to argue with her. I put on my jacket and followed her outside.

"Now, look," she said, "I'm a big girl and I can take care of myself. I don't know whether Sam told you or not, but I teach women's self-defense. I think it's wonderful, and very sweet, for you to be my knight in shining armor, but at the moment, your armor is in danger of rusting and we have to do something about it. The Chucks of the world grow up to do worse things. I'd like to be able to slow one down or maybe even stop him. And Mr. Chuck isn't going to get to first base with me. Oh, he's going to think he will, but no way. You know what a tease is, right?"

I nodded, feeling enormously relieved.

"Chuckie boy is going to meet the ultimate tease. I'm

going to have him going around in so many circles, he'll think he's stuck in a revolving door."

Better and better. I smiled. Knight in shining armor. I liked the sound of that.

"Now let's go in and map out the plan. Next week is a light one for me—two papers and a presentation this week— so the timing is perfect."

Mary had a middle school yearbook, and there were lots of pictures of Chuck. "He's not bad looking," Kara said with a mischievous smile at me. "Makes things easier. I wouldn't want to be gagging all the time."

We arranged for Mary to be at Chuck's locker before school started, with Kara hanging around near by. As soon as Chuck came and a positive identification was made, Mary would split. Kara would use Mary's locker, which was near Chuck's, as her own. Mary has this thing about combination locks and can't get the numbers right even when she has them written down in front of her, so she's never used her locker and carries everything around all day. Chuck would never suspect the locker wasn't Kara's. Mary gave her an extra JanSport knapsack she had. It was unlikely that Chuck would ever look in it, but Mary put a spare binder and some of her textbooks inside. Until this was over, she'd use mine.

During class periods, Kara would go to one of the girls' rooms and sit in a stall. If a teacher came in, she'd pull her feet up. I didn't like to think of her having to spend all that time in the bathrooms, but she said she didn't care where she studied and would probably get more work done than she would in her dorm room.

We were feeling pretty high. Monday was D-day and we all shook hands. I walked Kara to her car with a speech jumbled in my mind, sort of like the Academy Awards—"I can't thank you enough"—but I didn't get to say anything. I'd opened the door for her—Mom says it may be old-fashioned, but she still expects it, and it seemed to go over well with Kara, too—and she got into the driver's seat. She smelled great: shampoo and something else, lemony. "I—"

That was as far as I got. She smacked the side of her head. "Of course! Jack, I've just had the best idea. Now, chill. Everything's going to be fine."

"What is it?" I asked excitedly. Sam was so lucky to have a cousin like this. None of my cousins in California or New York remotely resembled Kara.

"I'm going to—no, better only I should know until it's all over."

She backed out of the driveway and I thought about

what my mother had said—that ADHD kids didn't worry about the future. Maybe I was getting better, or worse. All I knew was that for once, next week seemed very close and I was definitely worried.

chapter nineteen

THE NEW GIRL

The rest of the weekend sucked. My mother had told my father about the Life Skills quiz thing on Saturday morning. When I came home late in the afternoon, he was sitting in the living room and he was steamed. I honestly don't know why she waited so long. I'd forgotten all about it, of course. Whatever her reasoning, she'd told him, and that really pissed me off. It was totally unnecessary. She'd handled it. But she's always saying they don't keep things from each other, which we all know is a lie. Adults are always keeping things from each other. What she means is that *my* life is an open book, not hers or his.

Dad wasn't buying the whole ADHD future stuff any more than Mr. Hill or Mr. Margolis had. It was just me screwing up again, thinking I was soooo smart. That's just how he said it. Like Steve Martin, on old *Saturday*

Night Live reruns, except Dad wasn't funny. So I'm grounded, and if I ever fail another Life Skills anything, I'm going to a military academy. Dad has all these brochures and everything. Sometimes I think that this wouldn't be the end of the world. Boarding school. Not a military one, but just someplace where you wouldn't be hassled by your parents—and, more to the point, Chuck.

Mary and I have talked this over a couple of times. Her mother sometimes gets super crazed and tells Mary she simply cannot deal with her and can't keep her in the house—Mrs. Phillips's words. We've decided that while boarding school might have its advantages, home is best, because we mostly know what's going on. Besides, we'd miss each other, and the rest of our friends. I know my mother would never send me away, but I'm not so sure about Dad.

And with my luck, there would be another Chuck waiting.

Anyway, I did all my homework and then just had to sit around. I was supposed to be reading for English. We have to read one book a month for pleasure. It can be anything, the teacher said, but when I read a Mac manual for September, she wouldn't accept it, so now

I'm trying to get through *The Old Man and The Sea*. It's a pretty good book—short, and you really feel bad for the guy—but a lot of times I have to go back and reread what I've already read to keep things straight. Reading the manual was more pleasurable, but English teachers obviously don't think so. I wonder what Steve Jobs read when he was my age?

Mom and Dad went out Saturday night and Mom gave me the look and said she knew they could trust me not to touch the computer. I knew she'd check when she came home to see whether it was warm, so I had no problem agreeing. The telephone was off-limits, but if all my homework was done, I could watch TV. I ended up zoned out in front of a bunch of sit-coms, including a *Sabrina* rerun. There are a couple of shows that you can always find somewhere on cable, and *Sabrina* is one of them. I think the cat, Salem, is really funny. I couldn't help wishing I had some kind of powers, even though I knew the whole idea was stupid.

When I thought about what kind of powers—say, snapping my fingers and turning Chuck into a toad—the thought I kept having was doing something so I never had to take the pills in the first place. Slip through a wormhole, go back in time, and rearrange my molecules before I was born. That depressed me. I've never felt this way before. The pills were always just something I had to do. I went to bed early and was asleep when my parents came home. I thought teenagers were supposed to be the ones who got to go out and stay up late.

Sunday I had to do a million chores. My father was watching football games and my mother kept making me bring him stuff to eat. In her head, he was going to say something like, "Hey, son, forget the leaves and come sit next to your old man and we'll have a ball watching the tube." It's like the friendship-pool thing. You have to feel sorry for her. All this stuff that just isn't going to happen.

I was awake wicked early on Monday morning. I had this tingly feeling like Christmas morning, except this was totally different. I can't really describe it. Like what was going to be under the tree and will I break it all at once. Mom looked at me funny at breakfast. "Why are you in such a hurry, Jack? Is something going on I should know about?"

Absolutely not. No way. No, no, no.

"Nothing's going on. I promised Sam I'd meet him before school to talk about our science project." More lies. I was getting very good.

As I went out the door, Mom gave me my before-school meds. I rolled the pills around on my tongue as I ran for the bus. Fifty/fifty. I hoped it wasn't an omen.

Sam and I walked past Chuck's locker. Mary was talking to some girl, and I could see Kara reading notices on the bulletin board. No sign of Chuck himself, though. We walked straight ahead. Kara's ponytail was long and silky. She had a pink scrunchy that matched the shirt she was wearing.

I had to wait until seven o'clock at night before I found out how the plan had worked. Mercifully, my mom let me talk to Sam when he called. She probably thought it was about "the science project." I reminded myself to tell Sam we were doing one in case my mom brought it up.

"It's working!" Sam squeaked. "Kara just called and said he's already practically eating out of the palm of her hand."

I found this a gross and disgusting thought, but I kept my mouth shut.

"Not a single adult said anything to her, and she told the kids she met that she's just moved to town to live with her grandmother. She's making it seem like she was having problems with her parents and they sent her to live here. She told Chuck her grandmother is really strict and he can't come to the house, plus she has to be home immediately after school every day and can't go out on weekends until she proves that she's responsible. You know, the whole bad-girl thing. Chuck went for it hook, line, and sinker."

Again, I wasn't crazy for Sam's description, but I had to admit it was the perfect come-on. Was this what Kara had thought of as she was leaving on Saturday?

"Chuck's already told her about some of what he's been doing. All she had to do was say how much she loves to party—really party. He bragged he could get her anything she wanted. She kept making it seem like she didn't believe him and he spilled his guts. Kara thinks from what he said that you're the only kid he's taking pills from now, but he's planning to start with others. He takes some of the pills to get high himself and sells the rest or exchanges them for other stuff like pot, even coke, and I don't mean the drink."

I hadn't realized Chuck was into so much. Hell, the kid was an athlete. Didn't he worry about what he was doing to his body? I blurted this out to Sam.

"Come on, do you think you're the only kid who doesn't think about the future? Everything's gone fine for Chuck so far—and for his friends—so why shouldn't it just keep on?"

This made sense. Bad things didn't happen to them. Not yet, anyway, Chuckie boy.

"She'll string him along some more tomorrow, then she can't come on Wednesday. By Friday, she's sure she can get him to let her be there when he shakes you down."

I saw the two of them at lunch on Tuesday. Chuck was doing all these goofy things with some carrot sticks somebody's mother put in their lunch thinking how nutritional she was and not realizing that veggie stuff like that ends up in the trash or, in this case, coming out of Chuck's mouth like fangs. "Blood, I must have blood," he was saying in a pretty lame Count Dracula imitation. Kara was laughing like she thought he was funnier than *South Park*.

Dennis Smith and Linda Abernathy were sitting with them and Linda didn't look too happy. Dennis had grabbed some of the carrot sticks, too, and was tossing them at Kara like he was trying to get them down her shirt. One of the cafeteria workers started to come over and he stopped. I was glad Kara would be absent the next day and wouldn't be with the in-crowd. Linda was no dummy. I didn't want her to get jealous, start asking a bunch of questions, and maybe get suspicious enough to go to Mr. Dolan or something. I was definitely getting paranoid.

I wished the week would be over. I didn't know if I could stand the strain. On the way out of the caf, Chuck tipped Sam's tray over. Sam buys lunch and Chuck does this a lot. We don't even notice it much anymore, and when he does I give Sam my lunch, which I usually haven't eaten. Kara looked upset, then quickly started laughing. I knew it was a fake laugh. Chuck didn't.

On Wednesday Mary grabbed me as we left Club Meds. "In the hall this morning Linda Abernathy was talking about the new girl. How she's very stuck-up and was in all sorts of trouble at her old school. Linda says everybody should ignore her and not make friends with her. That she's not a good influence and is bound to give Busby a bad name."

I said it was too late, that Busby already had a bad name. I mean, what school is named "Busby"? Supposedly it was named after the old Busby farm that was torn down to build it. At the beginning of the year, when our history teacher was giving us a very boring history of the school, he said that it wasn't the Busby farm, but the Bunby farm. Either one sounds ridiculous to me.

"Come on, Jack!" Mary was annoyed. I had really spaced out. "This could screw everything up if Miss Perfect Abernathy starts going for Kara. I can just see Linda and her friends cornering Kara, asking a million questions. I mean, Kara is cool, but who knows what could happen?"

Maybe I wasn't paranoid, but I was, once again, clueless. "What can we do?"

"I'll call Kara and tell her what's going on. Maybe she can think of something." Kara had given each of us her phone number and e-mail, and told us to get in touch anytime, day or night. Saturday night when my parents were out, I had this urge to call her. I don't know why. I guess it's because I still can't believe she's doing this for me. I know what she said. That she's doing it for everybody in Club Meds and to make the future safe from Chuck, but I can't help feeling that she's also doing it just for me. Me, Jack Sutton.

Mary called late. Late according to Mom Time. Wow—it was almost nine o'clock. My mother said, "Give her the assignment and get right off. This is no time to be calling anyone. It's very late for Mary to be starting her homework too." As I've said, Mom is no fan of Mary's.

I grabbed the phone. Fortunately it was the portable and I took it upstairs to my room, where I told Mom I'd left my assignment notebook. Mary was talking fast. "Kara says she's not surprised. That Linda had been giving her dirty looks ever since they met and Dennis began to act like such a jerk. She says it's no big deal. She's going to talk to Linda tomorrow. Tell her how much she needs a friend like Linda who is obviously the most popular girl at Busby. And you know Linda won't be able to resist having someone like Kara at her heels and kissing ass."

"What about Dennis? Isn't Linda still going to be jealous?"

"Kara says she'll talk a lot about how great Chuck is and make it clear that she has no interest whatsoever in Dennis. She's going to make it seem that he's out of her league—that only a goddess like Linda is good enough for him."

Since this was probably what Linda thought, maybe Kara could get away with it.

"I think she's having fun. Kara, that is. She said she feels like she's in some teen magazine. She hated ninth grade. I can't imagine it, but she said she had braces, glasses, and wasn't at all popular. Getting to live it all over again looking the way she does now has got to be a trip."

I was sure Mary was exaggerating. Kara would look great even with braces and glasses.

"So there's hope for us all," Mary said.

At that point, my mother yelled up the stairs to get off the phone, so I said good-bye.

It was a good thought, though. Hope for us all?

chapter twenty

TITANIC

Kara was back in school on Thursday. I saw her walking through the halls with Chuck. She was wearing a pale blue sweatshirt and she was holding hands with him. Or he was holding her hand. It disappeared in that big hairy mitt of his. I was glad tomorrow was Friday and the whole thing would be over. Wherever I went I seemed to run into the gruesome twosome. They were in my lunch block again, and on the way out, Chuck stopped and said, "Tomorrow, same place, same time."

"Yeah," I answered, not bothering to raise my eyes.

"Hey, shithead, I expect you to look at me when I'm talking to you."

I started to lose it. I stood up and would have whaled into him, except the expression on Kara's face stopped me in time. I was sorry the rest of the day, though. Yes, I would have screwed up the whole plan, besides ending up a bloody, pulpy mess, but maybe I could have gotten a few punches in, maybe I could have hurt him.

Mary grabbed me as I was going into science. "Get a pass to the nurse and meet me under the stairs right away. We've got major trouble."

Mrs. Diamond gave me a pass and I headed for the stairs. Whatever architect designed the school didn't know kids—or maybe he did and was secretly sympathetic. There were these recessed areas under some of the staircases, and if you went all the way to the back, it was impossible for teachers to see you unless they came in too, which sometimes happened, but wouldn't now during class time. I knew which stairs Mary meant, because these places, like everything else at Busby, were strictly segregated. Just as you didn't go into certain bathrooms, you didn't go to another group's stairs. We didn't really have stairs of our own, but this one, not too far from the main office and the nurse, wasn't very popular. Like us. Figures.

Mary was waiting. "That dickhead Linda Abernathy told Miss Powers about Jessica, that is, Kara!"

I wasn't sure girls could be dickheads, but if they could, Linda was definitely one.

"Are you positive? And what would she tell? That

there's a new girl? Kara can lie low. It's only another day!" I wanted desperately to believe that our plan was going to work. That it would rain silver dollars and all the homeless people in the world would get houses.

"I guess Kara's sucking up to Linda didn't work. Linda is still out for blood. She must be worried that kids are going to like Kara better, especially Dennis. So little Miss Goody-Goody went to her coach and told her that she was worried about the kind of influence the new girl was going to have on the students at Busby, especially the ninth graders. That this new girl had been in a lot of trouble at her old school. I was in the bathroom and heard her tell the whole thing to her friend Courtney. Obviously they didn't know I was there. She is such a bitch!" Smoke was practically coming out of Mary's ears like a cartoon.

I wasn't getting it. Okay, so Linda told the cheerleading coach that there was a new student who'd had some problems at another school, but so what? It was just Linda, head cheerleader, brownnosing, making herself look superior.

"I don't see how this is going to matter. What can Miss Powers do?"

Mary interrupted me. "Dolt! You don't know what

girls are like at all! Besides telling Miss Powers that she was worried about Kara's wild ways tempting all us innocent little lambs at Busby, Linda told her she was worried about Kara, too. That she only wanted the new girl to have a fresh start. Fresh start, my ass! She wants to make sure the rep follows her here, not just with kids, but teachers, too. Courtney was laughing her head off. Linda even told Miss Powers that she thinks Jessica may need some counseling around sexual issues!"

Miss Powers taught one of the Life Skills sections. She'd leap at the chance to have a heart-to-heart with "Jessica." My heart sank. We'd hit an iceberg.

"Miss Powers said she'd find out who this Jessica's guidance counselor was and get on it right away. That she'd try to meet with her after school."

I was right. Miss Powers was as energetic as her cheerleaders. She wouldn't waste a moment. I could see her with one of those megaphones, running through the halls, calling, "Give me a 'J,' give me an 'E'. . . ."

This was too much to think about. "I've got to get back to class," I said. "She's giving a quiz the second half." It was on plate tectonics. I'd have no problem writing about the earth sliding around under the surface. My whole body felt that way.

We walked down the hall and I looked at Mary. The expression on her face wasn't encouraging. It was blank. Like someone had erased the board. "What are we going to do?" I asked.

A future without meds stretched before me. I'd start to fuck up in school. My parents would get on my case and eventually I'd have to tell them what had been going on and I'd really hear it for not telling them sooner, the old "It's not fair to me" thing. Sometimes I think my mother wants a diploma when I graduate too. I'd be facing the rest of this year and three more years of high school as a total outcast. I knew what would happen. Dog shit in my locker. Subtle stuff like getting pushed down the stairs and tripped in the halls. My notebook and textbook pages super-glued together. For starters, Chuck would break every bone in my body. I turned to Mary in total despair and asked again, "What are we going to do?"

"I don't know," Mary answered. We were in front of Club Meds. I had to get my pass signed by the nurse, invent something like a head or stomachache, lie down for a few minutes, and be miraculously cured. I knew Mrs. Diamond would ask for that pass. Mary's math teacher never did. "But I have to go tell Kara what's happened. She's in the girls' bathroom over by the auditorium. She'll have to leave the school right away."

"What about math?" I didn't want Mary to get in trouble.

"I'll tell him later that I got my period all of a sudden, and he won't want to go into it. Men like to pretend that menstruation doesn't exist."

Being a guy who doesn't really want to think about it either, I could see how this would work fine. I went into the nurse's office hoping she wouldn't look too closely at the time on the pass and I wondered, not for the first time, how it was that Mary could say anything to anybody.

The quiz was multiple choice—my favorite kind— and school was over. Mary and Sam were waiting by my locker. She'd obviously filled him in, because he was looking the way I felt. We'd come up with a good plan, but the Lindas in life always come up with better ones. And if she knew what she was *really* doing, she'd be awarding herself a medal. Chuck and her Dennis had been best friends since kindergarten.

"What did Kara say?" I asked.

"I told her what happened, and she had a few words for Linda. Then, before we could really talk, some other girls came in and she split. I said I'd call her tonight."

"Call me as soon as you talk to her," I said.

"Okay," Mary said.

We were walking out to the bus when we heard the announcement over the PA system.

"Jessica Ferris, report to the phys ed office immediately. Jessica Ferris, to the phys ed office." Jessica Ferris, a.k.a. Kara Gold.

We looked at each other. Not a single lifeboat in sight.

chapter twenty-one

STUNG

When I opened my locker door the next morning to put my jacket away, a tiny piece of paper fluttered out on to the floor. It was a note.

> *No matter what happens, be cool.*
> *—K.*

"Be cool?" Easy for Kara to say. I'd had almost no sleep the night before, and both my morning meds had been mints. Until I could get my Ritalin from the nurse, my brain would be doing a tap dance on the inside of my skull and I'd be praying it didn't show.

Last night had been the longest night of my life so far. Mary hadn't called while I was doing my homework, which I had expected, because Kara had said she wouldn't be available until the evening, so Mary wouldn't have reached her. But I still wanted to talk to Mary. Maybe she could pretend that everything was going to work out—just for my sake. I was going to ask her to give it a try, anyway. I planned to tell Mom I was calling Sam, but first we had to eat.

It was just Mom and me at dinner. Dad was away until Saturday. She was in a chatty mood, and I finally had to tell her I still had more homework, otherwise I'd have been there all night listening to what she wanted to do with *her* life. She wants to take some courses. I have no problem with Mom doing this if it will make her feel good. Also, it would mean she'd have her own homework and would maybe get off my back.

When I took the phone, Mom of course asked me who I was calling and why. That it was a school night—as if I could forget. I told her I needed to call Sam about the project, but she said it was too late, that Sam's mother had said he wasn't getting enough sleep and with his Bar Mitzvah coming up, it was very important he stay healthy. They'd had to postpone it a year because he'd had bronchitis and whatever he was taking got screwed up with his other meds and he missed too many Hebrew classes.

I'd been so busy worrying about my own life that I'd

pretty much forgotten about Sam's. Before all the Chuck trouble, Sam's Bar Mitzvah nerves were one of our main topics of conversation. I felt like a total jerk and *really* wanted to call Sam himself, then quickly call Mary. Mom said whatever I had to talk about would have to wait until the next day. I said it was only 9:30, but she said she didn't care. I yelled at her to stop treating me like a baby and slammed my door. Things were going great.

Mom came into my room and gave me my night meds. I kept them in my hand and put them under my pillow to take after I called Mary. There was no way she'd call now, and I *had* to find out what Kara had said. I told Mom I was really tired and was going to bed early, hoping she'd take the hint. I also told her I was sorry about slamming the door, which I was because I really don't like to fight with her. Especially since the person I was really mad at was me for totally forgetting Sam's Bar Mitzvah blues.

Then there was nothing to do but go to bed and wait. I wasn't sleepy at all, and apparently neither was Mom. At 10:30 I could see light coming out from under her door. She was still up. 10:45, then at 11:00 on the dot, she turned it out. I breathed a sigh of relief. Mary has a cell phone. Her grandmother gave it to her and her parents couldn't do anything about it.

I waited a while more to be certain Mom was asleep. She has amazing hearing and even now I wasn't sure I could get downstairs without her waking up and asking me what I was doing. I'd tell her I was getting a yogurt or something else to eat. This has happened before, though maybe not so late.

I crept out of my room. The hall and stairs are carpeted. I was sure I hadn't made a sound, but I waited in the downstairs hall half expecting her door to suddenly open. Then I went into the den and closed that door. The phone lights up at night. I never knew this. I punched in Mary's number and luck was with me. She picked up on the first ring.

"Jack," she said immediately. "I couldn't call. It was too late, but I was hoping you'd try."

I wasn't sleepy, but the room was cozy and dark. I imagined the phone line connecting the two of us, like the string between two tin cans—those telephones you make when you're a little kid.

"Don't get upset," she said, "but I haven't been able to reach Kara. I left a million messages on her cell. We'll have to think of something else."

Don't get upset. Mary couldn't see me. Tears were running down my cheeks. My nose was filled with snot.

"Yeah, well, see you," I managed to say.

"Jack!" Mary practically screamed into the phone. "Get a grip. We're not going to let this fucker win!"

Apparently Joan of Arc was back. I nodded and hung up before I realized that of course Mary couldn't have seen me. But it really didn't matter. Nothing mattered.

I put the phone back and went out into the hall again. Mom was still sound asleep. I went up to my room, swallowed the night meds, and still lay awake until dawn. I guess your mind has to be in sync with your body for the stuff to work.

And now there was this note. "No matter what happens, be cool." Was Kara in school after all? But that seemed crazy. If she got caught, she'd be in a lot of trouble. How would she explain what she was doing here at Busby? A college prank? Like a sorority thing? Passing for a high school kid to get into a club?

I put the paper in my pocket and by the end of the first block, it was almost in pieces because I'd reached in and taken it out to read so many times.

Second block we had an assembly. Don't ask me what it was about. Some people with musical instruments.

Drums, mostly. Joseph was next to me on the aisle.

"Today's the big day, right?"

"Would have been," I said. Sam must not have told him the latest.

Then Joseph said something I'll probably be thinking about the rest of my life. "It's not easy having a disability nobody can see, huh, Jack?"

The drums were kind of loud at that point and it wasn't the time or place for a heavy conversation, so I just said, "Thanks, buddy."

I could see Mary on the other side of the auditorium. She saw me and shook her head. I assumed that meant she hadn't been in touch with Kara. I wanted to take the note out of my pocket and wave it, but even off my meds I knew I'd look like a jerk.

All four of us were first in line at the nurse's office. She made a little joke about it and told us to have a good weekend. As soon as we were in the hall, Mary and I started talking at once. I told her to shut up and took out the note. I'd convinced myself that it meant that I was supposed to do my best to deal with a rotten situation. Like "Smile in the face of adversity." That's another of Mr. Schwann's sayings. He uses it when he passes back those tests on the horizon.

Mary had a totally different view. She was waving her hands around. "I knew she'd come through! Sam, your cousin is awesome. Something's going to happen when you go to give Chuck the pills, and whatever you do, don't blow it. Do what she says. Be cool."

Sam and Joseph brightened up.

"I think Mary's right," Sam said. "Kara has to be here, otherwise how did the note get in the locker? And she's going to go through with the plan. She'll be there to watch when Chuck takes your meds."

"But Mary said she isn't in any of the girls' rooms," I protested. I really wanted to believe them, but somehow I couldn't.

"She must have come early, seen Chuck, left you the note, and disappeared. After yesterday, she wouldn't want to take a chance that she'd get caught anywhere in the building," Joseph said reasonably. "She'll probably come at the end of the day and go straight to the equipment room."

"Why didn't she call you—or Sam?" I continued to worry. "Something's wrong. I feel it in my bones."

"Well, your bones are wrong—or maybe they're telling you it's going to rain," snapped Mary. "The best evidence we have is Chuckie himself. He's walking around today looking like he's won the lottery. He thinks they're going to be alone in the equipment room after you leave and all his dreams are going to come true. I'm sure he's told all his friends he's going to bag the new girl and she won't be able to get enough, stud that he is. . . ."

She would have gone on, but I told her to shut up again. I almost never talk this way to Mary, but she was making me crazy. At this point, my mind was flipping over and over. I didn't know whether I wanted Kara to be there or not.

Sam was looking as excited as Mary. "Kara's going to come back, I'm sure, and I can't see how anything can go wrong. I mean what's the worst that can happen? The three of you get caught and have to explain what you're doing in the equipment room. You can come up with something." I hadn't even considered this possibility, and now it was one more thing to worry about. What could I be doing there with the other two? Think, damn you, think, I said to myself, but nothing came. Sam was still talking and I forced myself to listen.

"But Chuck must be sure he's safe there, otherwise he'd have had you meet him somewhere else. And even if you did get caught, Kara would just say she's visiting, but then that would screw things up with Chuck. I mean, she'd have to tell him she doesn't go to school here or—"

"Stop it! Stop it right now!" I put my hands over my ears. I was feeling less and less in control these days. Yesterday I'd almost jumped on Chuck. And now I felt like my head was going to explode with all these scary thoughts. First Mary, now Sam. I thought about going to the nurse to get sent home.

But if I didn't show up, and Kara did come back, she wouldn't see me give Chuck the pills and that was the whole point of the grand scheme. That and whatever else had occurred to her in Mary's driveway. She'd see Chuck the total Puck and kind of blackmail him, but I had to be there.

Sam was looking at me with a strange expression on his face—pity, something like the way Mom looks when I've got the stomach flu.

"Why don't you tell the nurse you have a headache and lie down for a while?" he suggested.

"I'm fine. I'm absolutely, totally, completely fine," I yelled at him.

A few kids stopped and laughed at us.

"Sorry," I said. "I think I'm going insane."

"It's going to be okay," Sam said. Now he says it, I thought, but better late than never.

As soon as the bell rang at the end of the day, I went to my locker, threw my books in, and headed downstairs. For some reason I wanted my hands free.

Nobody was in the corridor and the equipment room was empty. I thought for a moment about hiding behind the door, but for what reason? It was all starting to be like a movie I'd never seen.

I heard their voices and walked out. Chuck had his arm slung around Kara's shoulders. She was smiling at him and didn't even glance my way. I was so happy to see her that it was all I could do to keep from *smiling* at her. But I wasn't supposed to be feeling happy. Not according to Chuck's plan.

"Well, well, look who's here. It must be the day they let all the freaks out of the loony bin." I backed into the room before he could push me in. Kara followed. She seemed bored.

"Is this going to take long?"

Chuck closed the door.

"Nah, as simple as one, two, three. Give me what you've got, asshole. Me and my lady have better things to do."

I took the envelope from my pocket and he counted

the pills, examining them carefully, then poured them into the film canister he'd taken from his knapsack. Kara was leaning against the door. She locked it. I heard the click. So did Chuck.

"Not yet, baby—"

Kara interrupted whatever he was going to say. "Oh yes, now, Chuck."

She pulled out a wallet and flashed him a badge.

"I've been undercover at Busby this week and you are in deep trouble, young man."

"Shit! Shit!" Chuck sank to the floor. "I can't believe this is happening! It's a joke, right! Come on, Jessica. You can't be a narc!" The canister with the pills rolled to one side. Kara picked it up.

"It's no joke," she said. I was confused for a second; Kara was a cop? Then my wires uncrossed and I was as cool as she had told me to be.

She looked at me. "Come over here, son. What is your name and how long has this been going on?"

I avoided Chuck and looked her straight in the eye. As far as I was concerned, it was all real. It seemed real. She was an undercover police officer and Chuck was going to be arrested.

"My name is Jack, I mean, John Sutton. This is the

second week that Chuck's taken my medication from me."

Kara looked at Chuck. "Besides being in possession of a controlled substance with intent to sell, you will be charged with violating John's civil rights and harassment. John, has he ever struck you or physically intimidated you in any way?"

I nodded.

"Then we can add assault to the charge as well."

Chuck suddenly came to life. "I want a lawyer." He watched a lot of TV.

Kara nodded. She had a notepad out and was writing everything down. "We'll go up to the office now and you can both call your parents."

Chuck's face became a mask of fear. "Parents? My parents can't know about this. My father will kill me. Really kill me. You've got to understand! You've got to help me." He started to cry. It was really ugly.

"You're a minor, Chuck. Your parents will have to be involved."

"Please, please, I'll never do anything like this again. It was mostly kidding. Jack knows that. Right, Jack?"

He grabbed my arm. He was begging. It should have felt good, but it didn't.

I kept quiet.

"Come on! I'm not the only kid doing stuff like this. Why don't you arrest them too! There are kids doing way worse things!" Chuck shouted.

Kara appeared to be lost in thought.

"We might be able to settle things here," she said, and sat down on a stack of mats in front of Chuck and motioned for him to sit too. "You're going to be an informant. I want the names of everyone you know in Busby and any other school in town who's dealing, anyone over twenty-one purchasing alcohol for you, and any other things that might occur to you that are against the law."

I went to the door to leave. I really wanted to get out of there.

"I need a witness. You'll have to stay here, John."

I sat with my back to the door and listened as Chuck sobbed out the list. There weren't too many surprises, but taken as a whole, it was sickening. When she finished, Kara told Chuck to stand up.

"You have something that doesn't come too often in life," she said, "a second chance. What you've been doing is as low as anything a person could do. You've been taking medication that is essential for John's health and well-being. And you've been endangering that of others, as well as yourself.

"I'll be keeping a close eye on you. You screw up even once and I'm going to be onto you so fast, you're never going to know what hit you. That means today, tomorrow, the next day, and for the rest of your sorry little life. No one is going to tolerate scum like you. Got it?"

Chuck nodded. He looked like he was going to heave.

"Now get out of here, both of you. Oh, yes, I almost forgot. Chuck, don't you have something to say to John?"

Chuck looked totally blank. He wasn't used to thinking this way. Then light dawned. "Uh, sorry. Sorry, Jack."

I didn't want to forgive him. And I didn't.

chapter twenty-two

THE END, SORT OF

It seemed like the entire membership of Club Meds was waiting in front of the school, not just Sam, Mary, and Joseph. It was the antennae again—everyone knew something was happening. I came out alone. Chuck had headed straight for the locker room, and much as I wanted to, I couldn't go back and talk to Kara. Mary came running toward me.

"What happened? Did it work? Tell us quickly, because we have to split before Chuck sees us all. But we had to wait."

"It worked," I said. I'd been feeling weird. Almost like crying, myself, then seeing everybody woke me up. "It worked!" I whooped and hugged Mary.

"What's going on?" a girl from my math class asked.

"Nothing," I said, "absolutely nothing. Isn't that great?"

"Nuts, totally nuts." She smiled and said she'd see me Monday. The group melted away until it was just the four of us gathered out of sight away from the front of the school. We were all grinning. We didn't know what to do. All we knew was, we wanted to do something together.

"Mochaccinos at Starbucks?" Mary said.

"Let's go for it," Joseph said. We never went to Starbucks. Only cool kids went there. Well, for the moment we were cool too. "Be cool," Kara had said. I hoped I had been.

Then suddenly there she was driving up in her little red VW Beetle. She was smiling as much as we were. We ran over to the car. She rolled down the window.

"I thought you might all be together," she said. "Here, Jack, you might need these." She tossed me my pills. "I don't want anyone to see me with you, so I've got to go. I'm sorry I couldn't talk to you last night. A good friend's boyfriend dumped her and she was in meltdown. I tried calling, but Mary's phone was busy and yours, too, Sam. What sounded definitely like a mom answered yours, Jack, and I hung up. Then it got too late. I e-mailed you, then remembered that sometimes you can't check it, so that's why I left you the note. Gotta run. Talk to you soon."

"Wait," I cried. "What about Miss Powers? What about Linda?"

"Oh, that was very funny. I'll fill you in when we have more time. Good old Linda. She's going to be one of those book-banning ladies, turning her neighbors in for God knows what. You guys were terrific. You came up with the perfect plan, and it worked!" She was gone.

We may have come up with the plan, but Kara had added the final touch and I'd realized in the room that without it, we might not have succeeded. As we walked to town, I told the kids what Kara had done. She'd been very careful not to say she was a police officer or that Chuck was under arrest. I don't think I've ever paid such close attention to anything anyone said in my whole life. Chuck had filled in the blanks, as she'd intended. And he'd be looking over his shoulder for years to come.

I'd like to say that school totally turned around for us and that all the Club Meds kids became the class officers, flavor of the week, popularity plus, but this is a true story. And maybe we don't want that, anyway. Mary says she doesn't. Kids still call us names, but not Chuck. We don't exist at all for him, especially me. He looks right through me.

I wanted to call Kara. I really missed her, and we'd

been through something together that I was always going to remember. Saturday night when my parents were out again—I was taking it as a good sign—I dialed her cell and she picked up. She's as easy to talk to as Mary, and after talking about a million different things, I asked her about what happened with Linda Abernathy and Miss Powers. What had Kara done? Just stay out of sight?

"That would have been nice, but I knew the moment Linda spotted me, she'd drag me off to the office or flag down a passing teacher and it was too risky to think she wouldn't see me yesterday. But it was really pretty easy. When I heard the PA on Thursday, I went to Miss Powers myself and told her who I was—Jessica the new girl. She started out by saying she hadn't been able to find out who my guidance counselor was, and I said no one had been assigned yet and right away thanked her for having me paged, because I was looking for an adult to talk to about the problems of being new in a school and how I wasn't even sure if I was going to stay, because I missed my family a lot, even though things hadn't been going smoothly. To make a long story short, I let her talk me into trying to go home and get some counseling help with my family. I was so into it, I began to believe I *was* Jessica. We both cried a little. She really cares about kids and I think she has Linda's number. I said something about not being too sure I could make friends here, because the girls hadn't been very welcoming and she said she wasn't surprised. She told me to stay in touch and gave me her extension at school. This morning I left her a message saying I'd moved back home. So exit Jessica, and it makes a great excuse for the kids other than Chuck."

I hadn't thought of that.

"Speaking of messages. Sorry the note wasn't longer, but I didn't have much time. I was up all night with my friend and had to get back to school for a class, and I needed to find Chuck to make sure we were still on for after school. Boy, was he on."

I had a couple of more questions. Like where did she get the badge and what did she plan to do with the list of names Chuck gave her?

"The badge was easy. I got it at a party goods place. It's for little kids—you know, birthday favors? You said the equipment room was pretty dark and I knew all I had to do was flash it. And what happened with the list is how I got the whole idea of being a cop in the first place. When I was leaving Mary's, I remembered Max—you met him at the lake, he's my brother—telling me that a friend of his is a probation officer. That this guy had trained to work with juveniles because he'd had a friend who had overdosed when they were teenagers. I figured if I could get Chuck to give me names, Max's friend could take it from there. The list has made its way to your cops now, I'm sure. They can't bust anybody without evidence, but they know who to watch. I'm not naive enough to believe that the scare I put into Chuck will last long. But the next time, he'll get caught for real and you'll be out of it."

"You're incredible," I said. It just slipped out.

"You're pretty incredible yourself, Jack. Take care and I'll see you around."

I didn't call her again. I didn't want to spoil it.

Maybe it was going back to full-strength meds again. I had a couple of minty days until the next month and a new prescription, but anyway, I finished the quarter in good shape, even Life Skills. Mr. Margolis wrote "much improved" in the comment column. I hate that word, "improved." Like we're all these donkeys stretching our necks out to get the carrots on the sticks.

Sam's Bar Mitzvah was a very big deal. The date has been circled in red in Sam's mind forever and the closer it got, the more crazed he got, even though I tried to calm him down. Learning Hebrew was really tough for him and he was sure he would blow it when he had to read his portion of the Torah. I sympathized with him. If I had to learn something like Hebrew on top of everything else, I'd be a goner. Not that I told Sam that.

I didn't see Kara at the temple, but she was at the reception afterward, which was in a private room at this very fancy restaurant. The kids were all sitting at their own table, and Sam was so happy it was over and he'd done fine that he forgot to be nervous that the place didn't have any windows. There was a band, and I felt a tap on my shoulder. It was Kara. Same lemony, shampoo smell. She had on a long black dress and looked terrific. Her hair was loose and swinging on her shoulders as she sang along to the music. "Killing me softly with his song . . ."

"Ever notice how they always play the same stuff at these things, Jack? Come on, dance with me."

I told her this was my first Bar Mitzvah, so I didn't know about the music, and she laughed. We didn't say much. I was concentrating on my dancing, but after a while I relaxed. She was really easy to follow. I know the guy is supposed to lead, but that's not my thing. Just before the song ended, she whispered in my ear, "Any more trouble?" I shook my head.

My mom and dad danced past us, looking like they practiced every night. I mean their steps matched perfectly. Mom had her head on Dad's shoulder. He looked at me, then at Kara, then straight back at me again. When her back was toward him, he grinned and gave me a thumbs-up. I think I was grinning back.

The music ended.

"See you," Kara said, and started back toward where she had been sitting.

"See you." I gave a little wave, then felt like a complete dork.

"Who was that?" My mother came up behind me.

"Just somebody I know."

"Honestly, Jack, all I did was ask you—"

My dad grabbed her. "Leave the kid alone, Diane, and come on, they're playing our song."

It was bad enough watching my parents make complete idiots of themselves on the dance floor, but since when had "Louie, Louie" been their song?

I danced some more, ate some stuff, and got to that point on the edge of being tired when you want to go home but don't want to admit it. I sat at one of the tables away from the music, looked around at everybody, and tried to put my thoughts into words I'd remember.

When you're a little kid, you think that your parents and teachers know everything about you. That all adults have a Vulcan mind-meld chip and can tell what you're thinking and doing all the time. There's a part of me that can't quite believe that nobody knew what was happening those weeks. My whole life changed, but to my parents it was as if nothing much was going on. I was getting up, going to school, coming home, going to bed. Eating in between.

I know now that there's a kind of invisible line everybody crosses when you start to have secrets. When what your life looks like on the surface has no resemblance to what's going on for real. Sometimes this really scares the shit out of me.

But sometimes this feeling that we all don't have to be stuck with the way we seem to be on the outside is great. I can sit in class or at home and think about who I am and what I know and feel pretty happy. I've even started looking ahead a little bit. I'll always be Jack Sutton or maybe John Sutton, but he's going to keep on changing. Then I feel free—like I ran down the hill fast enough and finally got off the ground.